Edward E. Hale

Historic Boston and its Neighborhood

Edward E. Hale

Historic Boston and its Neighborhood

ISBN/EAN: 9783337368197

Printed in Europe, USA, Canada, Australia, Japan

Cover: Foto ©Andreas Hilbeck / pixelio.de

More available books at **www.hansebooks.com**

APPLETONS' HOME READING BOOKS

HISTORIC BOSTON
AND ITS NEIGHBORHOOD

AN HISTORICAL PILGRIMAGE PERSONALLY CONDUCTED BY EDWARD EVERETT HALE

ARRANGED FOR SEVEN DAYS

Birthplace of Benjamin Franklin

NEW YORK
D. APPLETON AND COMPANY
1898

INTRODUCTION TO THE HOME READING BOOK SERIES BY THE EDITOR.

THE new education takes two important directions—one of these is toward original observation, requiring the pupil to test and verify what is taught him at school by his own experiments. The information that he learns from books or hears from his teacher's lips must be assimilated by incorporating it with his own experience.

The other direction pointed out by the new education is systematic home reading. It forms a part of school extension of all kinds. The so-called "University Extension" that originated at Cambridge and Oxford has as its chief feature the aid of home reading by lectures and round-table discussions, led or conducted by experts who also lay out the course of reading. The Chautauquan movement in this country prescribes a series of excellent books and furnishes for a goodly number of its readers annual courses of lectures. The teachers' reading circles that exist in many States prescribe the books to be read, and publish some analysis, commentary, or catechism to aid the members.

Home reading, it seems, furnishes the essential basis of this great movement to extend education

beyond the school and to make self-culture a habit
of life.

Looking more carefully at the difference between
the two directions of the new education we can see
what each accomplishes. There is first an effort to
train the original powers of the individual and make
him self-active, quick at observation, and free in his
thinking. Next, the new education endeavors, by the
reading of books and the study of the wisdom of the
race, to make the child or youth a participator in the
results of experience of all mankind.

These two movements may be made antagonistic
by poor teaching. The book knowledge, containing as
it does the precious lesson of human experience, may
be so taught as to bring with it only dead rules of
conduct, only dead scraps of information, and no
stimulant to original thinking. Its contents may be
memorized without being understood. On the other
hand, the self-activity of the child may be stimulated
at the expense of his social well-being—his originality
may be cultivated at the expense of his rationality.
If he is taught persistently to have his own way, to
trust only his own senses, to cling to his own opinions
heedless of the experience of his fellows, he is pre-
paring for an unsuccessful, misanthropic career, and
is likely enough to end his life in a madhouse.

It is admitted that a too exclusive study of the
knowledge found in books, the knowledge which is
aggregated from the experience and thought of other
people, may result in loading the mind of the pupil
with material which he can not use to advantage.

Some minds are so full of lumber that there is no space left to set up a workshop. The necessity of uniting both of these directions of intellectual activity in the schools is therefore obvious, but we must not, in this place, fall into the error of supposing that it is the oral instruction in school and the personal influence of the teacher alone that excites the pupil to activity. Book instruction is not always dry and theoretical. The very persons who declaim against the book, and praise in such strong terms the self-activity of the pupil and original research, are mostly persons who have received their practical impulse from reading the writings of educational reformers. Very few persons have received an impulse from personal contact with inspiring teachers compared with the number that have been aroused by reading such books as Herbert Spencer's Treatise on Education, Rousseau's Émile, Pestalozzi's Leonard and Gertrude, Francis W. Parker's Talks about Teaching, G. Stanley Hall's Pedagogical Seminary. Think in this connection, too, of the impulse to observation in natural science produced by such books as those of Hugh Miller, Faraday, Tyndall, Huxley, Agassiz, and Darwin.

The new scientific book is different from the old. The old style book of science gave dead results where the new one gives not only the results, but a minute account of the method employed in reaching those results. An insight into the method employed in discovery trains the reader into a naturalist, an historian, a sociologist. The books of the writers above named have done more to stimulate original research on the

Fourth Division. The fourth class of books includes more especially literature and works that make known the beautiful in such departments as sculpture, painting, architecture and music. Literature and art show human nature in the form of feelings, emotions, and aspirations, and they show how these feelings lead over to deeds and to clear thoughts. This department of books is perhaps more important than any other in our home reading, inasmuch as it teaches a knowledge of human nature and enables us to understand the motives that lead our fellow-men to action.

PLAN FOR USE AS SUPPLEMENTARY READING.

The first work of the child in the school is to learn to recognize in a printed form the words that are familiar to him by ear. These words constitute what is called the colloquial vocabulary. They are words that he has come to know from having heard them used by the members of his family and by his playmates. He uses these words himself with considerable skill, but what he knows by ear he does not yet know by sight. It will require many weeks, many months even, of constant effort at reading the printed page to bring him to the point where the sight of the written word brings up as much to his mind as the sound of the spoken word. But patience and practice will by and by make the printed word far more suggestive than the spoken word, as every scholar may testify.

In order to bring about this familiarity with the

printed word it has been found necessary to re-en-
force the reading in the school by supplementary
reading at home. Books of the same grade of difficulty with the reader used in school are to be provided for the pupil. They must be so interesting
to him that he will read them at home, using his time
before and after school, and even his holidays, for
this purpose.

But this matter of familiarizing the child with the
printed word is only one half of the object aimed at
by the supplementary home reading. He should
read that which interests him. He should read that
which will increase his power in making deeper
studies, and what he reads should tend to correct his
habits of observation. Step by step he should be
initiated into the scientific method. Too many ele-
mentary books fail to teach the scientific method because they point out in an unsystematic way only
those features of the object which the untutored
senses of the pupil would discover at first glance. It
is not useful to tell the child to observe a piece of
chalk and see that it is white, more or less friable,
and that it makes a mark on a fence or a wall. Scientific observation goes immediately behind the facts
which lie obvious to a superficial investigation.
Above all, it directs attention to such features of the
object as relate it to its environment. It directs attention to the features that have a causal influence in
making the object what it is and in extending its
effects to other objects. Science discovers the recip-
rocal action of objects one upon another.

After the child has learned how to observe what
is essential in one class of objects he is in a measure
fitted to observe for himself all objects that resemble
this class. After he has learned how to observe the
seeds of the milkweed, he is partially prepared to
observe the seeds of the dandelion, the burdock, and
the thistle. After he has learned how to study the
history of his native country, he has acquired some
ability to study the history of England and Scotland
or France or Germany. In the same way the daily
preparation of his reading lesson at school aids him
to read a story of Dickens or Walter Scott.

The teacher of a school will know how to obtain
a small sum to invest in supplementary reading. In
a graded school of four hundred pupils ten books of
each number are sufficient, one set of ten books to be
loaned the first week to the best pupils in one of the
rooms, the next week to the ten pupils next in ability.
On Monday afternoon a discussion should be held
over the topics of interest to the pupils who have
read the book. The pupils who have not yet read
the book will become interested, and await anxiously
their turn for the loan of the desired volume. Another
set of ten books of a higher grade may be used in the
same way in a room containing more advanced pupils.
The older pupils who have left school, and also the
parents, should avail themselves of the opportunity to
read the books brought home from school. Thus is
begun that continuous education by means of the public library which is not limited to the school period,
but lasts through life.   W. T. HARRIS.

WASHINGTON, D. C., Nov. 16, 1896.

CONTENTS.

xiii

LIST OF ILLUSTRATIONS.

2   xv

HISTORIC BOSTON
AND ITS NEIGHBORHOOD.

INTRODUCTION.

THIS little book is not so much a guide book in itself as an introduction or key to local guides, or a preparation for conversation with intelligent Boston people, who will meet a new comer into that town.

Every summer there arrive people from different parts of the nation who have a curiosity about the history of Boston, or about its present activities, which they would gladly gratify, as well as possible, in a few days' stay here. Perhaps they have ancestors among the fifteen thousand people who united in the capture of Louisburg, or the twenty thousand people who, thirty years later, defied King George. I recollect what I would gladly have done and said, first,

had my friends the Inghams and their children ever materialized far enough to appear
at the station in Park Square, and, second,
if my own deserts and desires had ever materialized so far that I could send my coach-
man and carriage to meet them. I have written to Colonel Ingham, the head of that little
host, the traveling directions which the reader
has in hand. At various places, if he need
them, as at Concord, at Lexington, or at
Cambridge, he will find local guide books
which will be of use to preserve, for memo-
randa which, at the moment, one has not time
to write down.

BEFORE leading the reader on any of the
separate excursions proposed, it will be well
that he should know something of the original make-up of the peninsula on which the
town of "Boston proper" has been built, for
the original Boston of the Fathers has been
enlarged by the filling in of coves and the
building of sea walls. The district north of
the line which separated old Boston from the

mainland has more than twice the area of
the "Neck," as they called it, which then
appeared above the water.

In our day we are apt to use the word
"neck" for the isthmus which connects a
peninsula with the mainland. Linguists may
interest themselves in observing the *connection* between *nexus*, the bond which unites
two bodies, and the *neck* which *connects* one's
head with his shoulders. In our earlier days,
however, the *Neck*, as a geographical term,
meant the whole peninsula. And on the New
England shore now people use the word in the
same way. Thus they speak of Marblehead
Neck, as the peninsula which a short neck between two coves connects with the mainland.
The phrase "Boston Neck" has of late days
been given only to the ridge of gravel which
connected the town with the mainland.

To the peninsula itself different names
were given by the early adventurers. It had
originally the outline of a 'fiddle—or, if you
please, of a pear. It projected northward
from the mainland, and on the other side

of the channel of Charles River, Charlestown, another "neck," not dissimilar, projected southward as if to meet it. Geologi-
cally each of the two peninsulas is a large
"drumlin," such as were left in all eastern
Massachusetts by the progress and by the re-
ceding of the great glacial wave which swept
over our part of North America somewhat less
than ten thousand years ago. In the *débris*
of this wave you pick up pebbles which have
been ground off from the rocks of the White
Mountains, and regions farther north than they.

Different observers of the olden times de-
scribe the peninsula in different ways. William Wood, an Englishman who came over
before 1630 and staid till 1635, says of it:

"His situation is very pleasant, being a
Peninsula hem'd in on the South side with
the Bay of Roxberry, on the North-side with
Charles River, the Marshes on the backe-side,
being not halfe a qvarter of a mile over; so
that a little fencing will secure their cattle
from the Woolves. Their greatest wants be
Wood and Medow-ground which never were

in that place; being constrayned to fetch their building-timber and firewood from the Islands in Boates, and their Hay in Loyters. It being a Necke and bare of wood, they are not troubled with the great annoyances of Woolves, Rattlesnakes, and Musketoes."

Edward Johnson, in the Wonder-Working Providence, wrote about 1650:

"The chief edifice of this City-like Towne is crowded on the Sea-bankes, and wharfed out with great industry and cost, the buildings beautiful and large, some fairely set forth with Brick, Tile, Stone, and Slate, and orderly placed with comly streets, whose continuall enlargement presages some sumptuous city. . . . But now behold the admirable Acts of Christ: at this his peoples landing, the hideous Thickets in this place were such that Wolfes and Bears nurst up their young from the eyes of all beholders, in those very places where the streetes are full of Girles and Boys sporting up and downe, with a continual concourse of people. Good store of Shipping is here yearly built, and some very faire ones."

In 1665 the Royal Commissioners, or some person employed by them, wrote in describing Boston:

"Their houses are generally wooden, their streets crooked, with little decency and no uniformity."

But Josselyn, who had been here but a short time before, said of the town:

"The houses are for the most part raised on the sea-banks, many of them standing upon piles, close together on each side of the streets as in London, and furnished with many fair shops; their materials are brick, stone, lime, handsomely contrived, with three meeting-houses or churches, and a town-house built upon pillars, where the merchants may confer; in the chamber above they keep their monthly courts. Their streets are many and large, paved with pebble stones, and the south side adorned with gardens and orchards."

The shape of the "drumlin" and its three hills has given the direction of the older streets, and determined the map of the present city. The settlers were not such fools as to suppose that streets must be straight, or that they must run along astronomical meridians or parallels. Where a street went in from the sea, it went at right angles from the shore or nearly so. Where Beacon Hill, or Copp's Hill, or Fort Hill rose, the roadway at the base went round them and not through them.

Given these preliminary streets—curves around the bases of the hills, and radii, so to speak, running from the water's edge to meet them—run the main street north, midway between the shores of the coves, and you have the key to what a stranger calls the intricacy of the streets of the town.

The winding line of the shore, deeply indented by coves, suggested at once operations for artificial embankments. The rise and fall of the tide is from eight to twelve feet. It occurred to the settlers very early that by making a causeway, where Causeway Street now runs, and adjusting gates to open inward, and close when the water flowed out, a mill basin could be made from the great northern cove, and kept nearly at the level tide. They therefore built this causeway, and thus, by cutting a narrow canal eastward across the town, they commanded, perhaps half the time, a waterfall from the high tide level to that of low tide, sufficient to carry a mill for grinding their corn. The tide basin thus made was called the Mill Pond.

In 1804 it was clear that the land it covered would have value, if reclaimed, of much more account than the little water power which had been used for nearly two centuries. Enough of Beacon Hill was cut down, therefore, to fill up the Mill Pond. The canal was filled up, and became Canal Street. Here is the reason why, in the heart of the devious plan of the North End, there come in straight streets which mark the site of the original Mill Pond. And thus the original Beacon Hill lost its crest, which rose behind the State House of that day.

At the same time the old enterprise for creating tide power was renewed on the Back Bay. The region of elegant houses now known as the Back Bay was then really the

The Public Garden.

bay, back of the town to one who approached it from the sea.

By building the Western Avenue across this bay—from Beacon Street exactly west to Brookline—a basin was located, in which the water could be kept at any level. Southward across this basin a mill dam was built, which is now Parker Street, and thus there were two basins. The western of these two, about where the Charlesgate Fens now are, was kept nearly at the level of high tide, and was called the "full basin." The eastern basin was kept at the lowest level possible, and was called the "empty basin." From the full to the empty basin was an average waterfall of salt water of perhaps eight feet. The water power thus created carried several mills. My father had printing presses there, which were kept at work by the use of this power.

By this cutting off of the high tide from the foot of the Common, the present parade ground was created, where till then there had been only an unsightly salt marsh. And Charles Street, on a causeway again, was extended south from Beacon Street to Park Square.

All this was done under the mayoralty of the first Quincy. The trees now making so fine an avenue of the Charles Street Mall were planted then. Virtually the Common was almost doubled in size by these improvements. Fifty years ago, under the masterly lead of Mr. Samuel E. Guild, the Public Garden was created on what had been an unsightly beach of salt mud on the western side of Charles Street.

When in 1831 the construction of the Worcester and Western Railway was made certain, another set of adventurers filled up the "South Cove," which indented the shore on the east side. Here again, therefore, is a series of rectangular and level streets. Washington Street curves as the crest of the old isthmus curves. In the old days it was the only street between the South Cove on the east and the Back Bay on the west.

Go through Union Park Street from Washington, and turn in by the side of the

Temple Shalom. You can see from the steps the remains of a wooden wharf where your grandfather bought cabbages and firewood "imported" from Maine. The Temple Shalom stands where the schooner lay from which they were landed.

The traces of this history are found by the pilgrim on the spot and in the names of streets and squares. Beacon Street commemorates the beacon which was ready to summon the soldiers of the bay in the event of any attack. General Gage was sadly frightened when he received a report one morning that a tar-barrel had been found in the iron basket of the beacon. I can not find that the beacon was ever really fired. And here I may say that, of six forts built in succession where Fort Independence now stands, no one ever fired a shot in anger. But the tower of Brattle Street Meeting House preserved to the last an iron cannon ball which struck it in a cannonade ordered by Washington in the siege of Boston. Mr. Holmes's lines on this are these:

" Wears on her bosom as a bride might do
The iron breastpin which the rebels threw."

The Brattle Street Meeting House.*

Fort Hill was dug away to a level a generation ago, but a pretty circle of grass preserves the name, though there be no hill.

The reader may now safely be trusted to
go out from the center on the excursions described in these letters.

* Observe the cannon ball over the doorway.

I.

WARS AND RUMORS OF WARS.

CRANBERRY CENTER, *July 20, 1898.*

MY DEAR COLONEL INGHAM: I have your letter too late, alas! to meet you at the train. But William will meet you with this, and take you to the house directly. Meanwhile, you will want to be showing the lions to your wife and to those fine boys. Take this letter with you as your marching guide.

If I know those boys of yours, they will be eager, first of all, about Lexington and Concord and Bunker Hill. Why do you not take their broad hints, and at the same time indulge your wife's curiosity about the homes of Emerson, and of Hawthorne, where she will now find Mrs. Lothrop, and where even the "hack-driver" will tell her stories of Thoreau?

Indeed, if you break this open before you

3   13

leave the station, you can send Mrs. Ingham and the trunks to our house, and you and the children can start on foot.

For, in a sense, when you meet William at the Providence station, you are all standing where you might have been swimming when and where the battle of Lexington began. That was all water then, and you must impress it on the boys that near that spot the boats from King George's squadron met quietly to forward the regiments detached for a surprise excursion on the evening of the 18th of April, 1775. You may as well take the boys with you through Arlington Street to Beacon Street and then to the Union Boat Club House. Impress it on them, all the way, that this was all under water then, and that after dark, on that eventful April evening, rather more than a thousand soldiers were being rowed by the seamen of the fleet to East Cambridge—what they then called Phips's Farm. Go in from Beacon Street through a little street they call Otter Street, and

almost directly north, nearly parallel with
the present land line, these thousand men
were taken thus across the mouth of Charles
River. The bridge to Cambridge—what Mr.
Lowell calls one of our "caterpillar bridges"
—crosses their line. But I think you can
see a steeple and a chimney on the East
Cambridge shore above that bridge.

Do not go any farther with them then,
but take them back to the house, and as soon
as their mother is ready, after breakfast, you
can all start for Lexington and Concord, on
the line on which Lord Percy followed the
first detachment. The boys will know that
he went the next day.

I do not know how you feel about money.
It is well worth what a carriage will cost
you. But if I had your legs and the boys', I
would do it all, with the help of the trolleys
and the steam cars, for half a dollar apiece.
Let that be as madam says.

Percy's brigade slept that night in their
tents on the Common. And if you choose
you can walk across on the broad path from

the Providence station to West Street over
the very line of his little camp. With these
eyes I have seen the rings, in the green grass
of the spring, which showed where his tents
were. Colonel Smith had been sent out with
his thousand men as a sort of surprise, by
night. But he sent word back that the country was alarmed, and Percy was directed to
take a large detachment to his relief. Percy
was a fine young fellow, a spirited soldier,
son of the Duke of Northumberland, whom
he succeeded afterward in the dukedom. He
was half-brother, by another mother, of that
James Smithson who founded the ·Smith-
sonian Institution. Perhaps the name Smithson is now better known than that of Percy
among English-speaking people; certainly
James hoped it would be. Percy paraded
his men early and marched them out from
the Common to what we call Tremont Street,
and there they were drawn up across the
head of School Street, all ready to march,
but that he had to wait for the detachment of
marines from the fleet who were to join him.

LINE OF THE MINUTE MEN
APRIL 19   1775

STAND YOUR GROUND
DONT FIRE UNLESS FIRED UPON
BUT IF THEY MEAN TO HAVE A WAR
LET IT BEGIN HERE

CAPTAIN PARKER

Bowlder on Lexington Common.

" Where are those marines? "

Where, indeed! At last an orderly was summoned, who stated, with true British precision, that he had left the order for Major Pitcairn, the commander of the marines, at his headquarters the evening before. And four hours before this Major Pitcairn had said to the militia on Lexington Green, " Disperse, ye rebels, disperse!" and war had begun. And now his orders are lying sealed on his office table, and he is far away!

As soon as this was found out somebody else got the marines into line, and the column moved out of town over the Neck, exactly away from Concord, where they were going, as the bird flies, but through another country from Colonel Smith's route, so that they might astonish the natives.

Let Mrs. Ingham and the boys understand this. By the way, as you go out, following Lord Percy after one hundred and twenty-two years, you pass between two pretty squares, east and west of Washington Street. Tell the boys that here were the farthest redoubts held by the English troops. Dr. Weld told me he had often driven his father's cows over them. Ask the driver or conductor to show you the old burial ground at Eustis Street.

Go up the hill to the Norfolk House and Center Street. At Center Street is the "parting stone." Your road is the Cambridge road, the other road is the Rhode Island road.

Now you must leave your car, if you are in it. If you are in a carriage, tell the driver to go to Brookline. If you walk, you have only to go down the hill, and at the great arches of the Providence Railway take a Brookline car. Tell the conductor that you want to go through Harvard Street. Or tell the driver you want to go to Cambridge by the old road, crossing the river by the old bridge at Cambridge.

Now you are on Percy's line of march. Somewhere here in Roxbury his band was playing "Yankee Doodle." Percy saw a boy deriding the column by shouts and gestures, and called him to scold him. "You go out

to Yankee Doodle," said the boy, "but you
will come back to Chevy Chase!" And Dr.
Gordon, who tells the story, says that the
boy's words haunted Earl Percy all day.

> The child may rue that is unborn,
> The hunting of that day.

If anybody knew that ballad, " Erle Percy " did.

Rather more than two miles from the
parting stone you will pass the old " La-
fayette Tavern " on your left, and in half a
mile more will be in sight of the Cambridge
boathouses and will have Charles River to
cross.   Earl Percy came there as you do, but
the American General Heath had ordered
that the planks of the little bridge should be
taken up to check him.   So the earl found
no bridge.   But alas, the Yankees had not
yet learned what war is !   They had frugally
piled the planks on the Cambridge shore.
If they had thrown them into the river
Smith's detachment would hardly have returned to Boston that night.

As it was, Percy put men across to lay
the bridge again, and after a tedious delay
he crossed with his "army," which had now
marched eight or more miles. You are only
three miles from Boston by the road of to-
day.

Stop, if you like, in Cambridge, at Gore
Hall and ask for some of the old Revolutionary maps and pictures. Gore Hall is the
college library, and they will be very courteous to you. Make a stop for lunch at the
trolley station in Harvard Square.

Your next objective is Arlington, once
West Cambridge, and in Percy's days Menotomy. Percy was confused when he came
up to the town of Cambridge from the
broken bridge. Nobody appeared to tell
him the way, but a poor college tutor was
caught, whose name I may repeat, as it was
Smith. He could not tell a lie, and he
directed the commander to Menotomy; for
which offense against liberty he was ostra-
cized by the people and had to retire to Halifax for eight years.

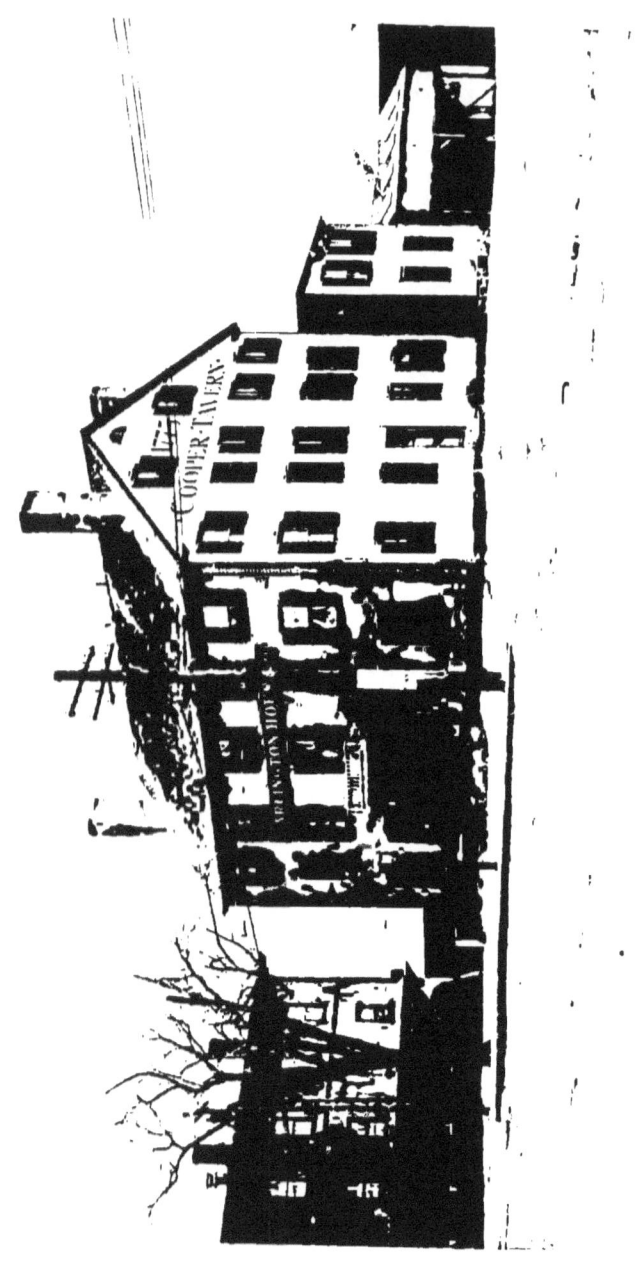

You have had a trolley, or a good road, to Arlington. At Arlington you will find a tablet which shows where the first victory of the war was won—unless you count the Boston boys' victory about the sleds and the coasting. For here, under the lead of an old negro soldier, the "exempts" of Menotomy cut off Percy's supply train, the meat (and drink) for his little army. This essential of war had been detained at the bridge. So the first real victory of the war was won by a black man. It was at Menotomy, now Arlington, that Percy first learned that fighting was going on beyond.

I once made the excursion which I am describing to you, on the 19th of April. On that day you will see a flag on every old-fashioned house between Arlington and Lexington. And if you stop at the door of any such house, you will be asked if you do not want to see where Cephas Willard died, or somebody else. Or would you like to see the blood stain on the floor, or the bullet in a beam? These people are

proud of these memories and preserve their
memorials.

It is not a long march or ride to Lexington. There, on the hill southeast of the village, Percy met the flying column of Colonel Smith. Smith was himself wounded,
and was in a "chaise" which had been im-
provised for the purpose. He disappears
from history from this time. Percy unlim-
bered his cannon, and, when he got a chance,
fired a round shot up the road. I think they
show one or two of these balls in the Public
Library of Lexington.

For you will find the public library open
and hospitable, and ready to tell you and
show you everything. It is on the right-
hand side of the road. Among other things
they will show you a portrait of Lord Percy,
which the present Duke of Northumberland
sent them. He was very much pleased when
Rev. Mr. Porter told him that the Lexington
people sometimes spoke of "our Lord Percy."
By the way, Percy's letters home to his
father and mother are among the most life-

like memorials which we have of that winter.
Poor fellow, he got enough of campaigning
under that lazy Sir William Howe, and went
back to England. He did not appear as a
soldier again until as Duke of Northumberland he commanded the volunteers who were
expected to drive away Napoleon when he
made the descent which never came on the
English shore. All the Percys were Smith-
sons by name, Lord Percy's father being
only the third duke of this creation. The
Dudley line of Dukes of Northumberland
had run out in another century, or had been
beheaded.

With the boys fairly landed in the library, and a walk up to the "center" of the
town to see the monument and to read the
inscription, I am afraid these instructions will
end. Though if you are "doing the thing"
as an English traveler would do it, you
would include Concord, Bunker Hill, Harvard College, and the House with Seven
Gables in the same day. As it is, I will
have mercy on you, and let you come home.

There will be some music somewhere in the evening. Indeed, you will find Boston a good watering place.

If mamma is too tired to take the children out in the evening, you, Fritz, may read the ballad of the New England Chevy Chase aloud to the rest; and then Pauline may commit it to memory, to recite at the next meeting of the Great Granddaughters of the Revolution. Here it is:

NEW ENGLAND'S CHEVY CHASE.

'Twas the dead of the night. By the pine-knot's red
    light
Brooks lay, half asleep, when he heard the alarm—
Only this, and no more, from a voice at the door:
    "The Red-Coats are out, and have passed Phips's
      farm."

Brooks was booted and spurred; he said never a
    word;
    Took his horn from its peg, and his gun from the
      rack;
To the cold midnight air he led out his white mare,
    Strapped the girths and the bridle, and sprang to
      her back.

Up the North Country Road at her full pace she
    strode,
    Till Brooks reined her up at John Tarbell's to say,

" We have got the alarm—they have left Phips's
    farm ;
You rouse the East Precinct, and I'll go this way."

John called his hired man, and they harnessed the
    span ;
They roused Abram Garfield, and Abram called
    me :
" Turn out right away ; let no minute-man stay ;
The Red-Coats have landed at Phips's," says he.

By the Powder-House Green seven others fell in ;
    At Nahum's the men from the saw-mill came
    down ;
So that when Jabez Bland gave the word of com-
    mand,
    And said, " Forward, march ! " there marched for-
    ward The Town.

Parson Wilderspin stood by the side of the road,
    And he took off his hat, and he said, " Let us pray !
O Lord, God of Might, let thine angels of light
    Lead thy children to-night to the glories of day !
And let thy stars fight all the foes of the Right
As the stars fought of old against Sisera."

And from heaven's high arch those stars blessed our
    march,
    Till the last of them faded in twilight away ;
And with morning's bright beam, by the bank of the
    stream,
    Half the county marched in, and we heard Davis
    say :
4

" On the King's own highway I may travel all day,
  And no man hath warrant to stop me," says he ;
" I've no man that's afraid, and I'll march at their
    head."
  Then he turned to the boys—" Forward, march !
    Follow me."

And we marched as he said ; and the fifer he played
  The old White Cockade, and he played it right
    well.
We saw Davis fall dead, but no man was afraid ;
  That bridge we'd have had, though a thousand men
    fell.

This opened the play, and it lasted all day.
  We made Concord too hot for the Red-Coats to
    stay ;
Down the Lexington way we stormed, black, white,
    and gray ;
  We were first in the feast, and were last in the
    fray.

They would turn in dismay, as red wolves turn at
    bay.
  They leveled, they fired, they charged up the
    road.
Cephas Willard fell dead ; he was shot in the head
  As he knelt by Aunt Prudence's well-sweep to load.

John Danforth was hit just in Lexington Street,
  John Bridge at that lane where you cross Beaver
    Falls,
And Winch and the Snows just above John Munroe's,
  Swept away by one swoop of the big cannon balls.

Monument on Lexington Common.

I took Bridge on my knee, but he said, " Don't mind
    me ;
Fill your horn from mine—let me lie where I be.
Our fathers," says he, " that their sons might be free,
    Left their king on his throne and came over the
    sea ;
And that man is a knave or a fool who, to save
His life for a minute, would live like a slave."

Well, all would not do ! There were men good as
    new—
    From Rumford, from Saugus, from towns far
    away—
Who filled up quick and well for each soldier that
    fell ;
    And we drove them, and drove them, and drove
    them all day.
We knew, every one, it was war that begun,
When that morning's marching was only half done.

In the hazy twilight, at the coming of night,
    I crowded three buckshot and one bullet down.
'Twas my last charge of lead ; and I aimed her, and
    said,
    " Good luck to you, lobsters, in old Boston Town."

In a barn at Milk Row, Ephraim Bates and Munroe
    And Baker and Abram and I made a bed.
We had mighty sore feet, and we'd nothing to eat ;
    But we'd driven the Red-Coats, and Amos, he said :

" It's the first time," says he, " that it's happened to
    me
    To march to the sea by this road where we've come ;

But confound this whole day, but we'd all of us say
  We'd rather have spent it this way than to home."

————

The hunt had begun with the dawn of the sun,
  And night saw the wolf driven back to his den.
And never since then, in the memory of men,
  Has the old Bay State seen such a hunting again.

II

BUNKER HILL.

IF all this be not enough of wars and rumors of wars, there is a nice little afternoon expedition which the young people can take by themselves while Papa and Mamma are writing their letters or taking their naps.

It is the journey by land to Fort Independence, which is on an island—Castle Island.

As long ago as 1631, when Governor Winthrop brought the first colonists to Boston, he saw that he should defend the harbor best by a fort on what was called Castle Island. All the towns in the little State were taxed to build the "Castle," and it was finished well enough to have cannon on it in 1634. Between that time and this, six forts have been built there and opposite it. There will be time for this another day. But now the boys

will wonder that they have not been to Bunker Hill. Of course they saw the monument
very early in the business. Did not Paul
repeat—

"Let it rise till it meet the sun in his
coming! Let the earliest rays of morning
gild it, and let the parting day linger and
play upon its summit!"

But all of the youngsters will want to
trudge up to the top and count the steps. I
think mamma will prefer to attend the meeting of the "Granddaughters of Queen Anne's
Counselors," and that papa will have a business engagement with Sewall and Saltonstall
about some wheat he has off Tierra del Fuego.

Very well! Off with you, and even if
you have English tongues, still you need
not ask anybody where to go. Just show
yourselves on Tremont or Washington Streets,
and look at the electrics northward bound
till you see one marked

"BUNKER HILL!"

Somebody complains because he does not
like to find *Tintagel* in Bradshaw's Guide. I

may say, in passing, that it is not there, for I have looked for it. But I never complain when I see BUNKER HILL on a car, even if I have no business there, as General Howe and Major Pitcairn had. It does one good to be taken back a hundred and twenty-three years or thereabouts.

Enter the car bravely, and affect to know the whole way. Let us hope you all know that the sun is in the south at noon and in the west in the afternoon, so that you shall not travel southward to Roxbury. You shall go to see General Ward's forts there another day.

Where you cross this bridge there was a ferry the day the battle was fought—yes, and for one hundred and forty-five years before. It was there, Jane, that your grandmother's grandfather and his wife came over with Winthrop in 1630. They all came first to Charlestown, where we are going now. And there your great-great-grandfather began a little hut, something like Nansen's, on the side of the hill. But they sickened there; they had no good water. And one day a man named

William Blaxton came over from the Shawmut, where you are making your visit, now called Boston. And he told them that over there he had good water, and so your ancestor, and perhaps twenty-five more like him, with their wives and babies, went over. And this made the beginning of a ferry way which lasted till this very bridge was built—oh, fifteen years or so after the battle.

It was across here that Paul Revere came in his little boat before the battle of Lexington, as you have read in Mr. Longfellow's ballad of Paul Revere's Ride.

On through the "Square," which, like most Boston squares, has more than four corners, and here the motorman says, "Far'z we go," and we see that we can walk right up the hill to the monument.

It is not very far, Paul, from the slope where Major Abercrombie led up his redcoats, and heard some one from the other side of the breastwork cry out:

"Are the Americans cowards, Major Abercrombie?"

The Battle of Bunker Hill.
From Trumbull's painting.

And here we are, with the great stone obelisk above us. And here is the door. The chances are good that the keeper can tell us all about it. In some years there is an elevator running to take us up; in some years no. Who cares, if we are more than eight years old and not yet twenty? We shall like to count the stairs.

Ask the doorkeeper if he have General Devens's address, delivered in General Grant's presence, on the anniversary of the battle. If he has, buy it. It will tell you the whole story.

When you come home at night tell the old folks what you have seen. This time there shall be two ballads. Here is a verse from one by a Yankee soldier. I am afraid he was not in the trenches:

THE BALLAD OF BUNKER HILL.

We lay in the trenches we'd dug in the ground
   While *Phœbus* blazed down from his Glory-lined
      Car;
And then from the lips of our *Leader* renowned
   This Lesson we heard in the *Science* of War!

"Let the Foeman draw nigh
Till the *White* of his *Eye*
Is in range with your *Rifles*, and then, *Lads!* Let
Fly!
And show to *Columbia*, to *Britain*, and *Fame*,
How *Justice* smiles awful when *Freemen* take Aim!"

Now, this other one is not so good for poetry, but it is genuine. I print it from the old yellow "broadside," as such things are called. It was printed in Boston, I suppose to encourage recruiting in the British army:

Reproduction of cut from the original "broadside."

A SONG,

COMPOSED AFTER THE FIGHT AT BUNKER HILL, JUNE 17, 1775.

It was on the seventeenth by brake of day,
The Yankees did surprise us,
With their strong works they had thrown up,
To burn the town and drive us;

But soon we had an order come,
  An order to defeat them:
Like rebels stout they stood it out
  And thought we ne'er could beat them.

About the hour of twelve that day,
  An order came for marching,
With three good flints and sixty rounds,
  Each man hop'd to discharge them.
We marched down to the long wharf,
  Where boats were ready waiting;
With expedition we embark'd,
  Our ships kept cannonading.

And when our boats all filled were
  With officers and soldiers,
With as good troops as England had,
  To oppose who dare controul us;
And when our boats all filled were
  We row'd in line of battle,
Where show'rs of balls like hail did fly,
  Our cannon loud did rattle.

There was Cop's hill battery near Charlestown,
  Our twenty-fours they played,
And the three frigates in the stream
  That very well behaved;
The Glasgow frigate clear'd the shore,
  All at the time of landing,
With her grape shot and cannon balls
  No Yankee e'er could stand them.

And when we landed on the shore,
    And drew up all together;
The Yankees they all man'd their works,
    And thought we'd ne'er come thither:
But soon they did perceive brave Howe,
    Brave Howe, our bold commander,
With grenadiers, and infantry,
    We made them to surrender.

Brave William Howe, on our right wing,
    Cry'd, boys fight on like thunder;
You soon will see the rebels flee
    With great amaze and wonder.
Now some lay bleeding on the ground
    And some full fast a running
O'er hills and dales and mountains high,
    Crying, zounds! brave Howe's a coming.

They began to play on our left wing,
    Where Pegot he commanded;
But we return'd it back again
    With courage most undaunted.
To our grape shot and musket balls,
    To which they were but strangers,
They thought to come in with sword in hand,
    But soon they found their danger.

And when the works they got into,
    And put them to the flight, sir,
Some of them did hide themselves,
    And others died with fright, sir.

Bunker Hill Monument.

And then their works we got into
   Without great fear or danger,
The work they'd made so firm and strong:
   The Yankees are great strangers.

But as for our artillery
   They all behaved dinty;
For while their ammunition held,
   We gave it to them plenty.
But our conductor he got broke
   For his misconduct, sure, sir;
The shot he sent for twelve-pound guns
   Were made for twenty-four, sir.

There's some in Boston pleas'd to say,
   As we the field were taking,
We went to kill their countrymen,
   While they their hay were making;
For such stout Whigs I never saw;
   To hang them all I'd rather,
For making hay with musket-balls,
   And buck-shot mixed together.

Brave Howe is so considerate,
   As to prevent all danger;
He allows half a pint a day;
   To rum we are no strangers.
Long may he live by land and sea,
   For he's beloved by many;
The name of Howe the Yankees dread,
   We see it very plainly.

And now my song is at an end ;
And to conclude my ditty,
It is the poor and ignorant,
And only them, I pity.
As for their king John Hancock,
And Adams, if they're taken,
Their heads for signs shall hang up high
Upon that hill call'd Bacon.

III

JOHN ELIOT AND HIS INDIANS.

To Mrs. Frederic Ingham—Dear Polly: I understand what you say, and I have read between the lines. That tall Polly of yours will be at meetings of "Colonial Dames" and "Daughters of the Pyrates," and I do not know what other conclaves, when she gets home, and she wants to talk literature. She will want to say that she has seen the home of this author and walked in the footsteps of that.

Dear child, she shall. And you and I will lead her.

She knows, and you know and I know, that the first absolutely first-rate work done in a literary way here was John Eliot's work —the dear Indian apostle. He was really a very remarkable man. Do you know that

when the great linguists of this century got
to work, the people we call philologists now,
the Grimms, the Duponceaus, the Brintons,
and the rest of them, when they buckled
down to old John Eliot's studies of the Indian
language they found he understood his business as well as the best of them, and did as
clean and thorough a bit of work as ever was
done? That speaks pretty well for his Jesus
College, at Cambridge, and pretty well for
the grit of the dear old fellow himself.

Nobody has any excuse for ignorance
now, for Eliot's admirable successor, one of
to-day's apostles, Dr. De Normandie, has
written out all Eliot's history. I have the
paper before me as I write, and I shall send
it to your Polly. This letter, in fact, is all
taken from it. You will find it in the New
England Magazine, where there is so much
else which a traveler values.

It is only as far as the little statue in a
niche, where Roxbury Street leaves Washington Street, that you will follow Percy's
march, where you went when you were seek-

ing battle memories. And now practically your "Eliot pilgrimage" will be over new ground. Look at the little statue in the niche—remember that Percy took the road to the right, and do you go to the left as far as the People's Bank. A little behind the People's Bank stood the parsonage where John Eliot lived from the month of November in the year 1632, when he came to be "teacher" of the First Church in Roxbury, where Thomas Weld had already been chosen "minister and pastor." Young Eliot had graduated at the English Cambridge in 1623, having studied at Jesus College. Let us hope that that society knows enough to count him in the front company of its noblest sons. Eliot had married, only the month before, the lady whom he called his "ancient dearly beloved wife " fifty-three years afterward.

While your husband goes upstairs to the bank to ask for change for a bill, you can "dilate with the right emotions," as Mr. Choate said. You and the children can look northward to the new block of stores, where

Mr. Norton has his furnace and stove shop.
On that corner General Artemas Ward, the
first commander of the Continental army, had
a little fortification, the guns of which commanded the street over which you have come,
so that the English could not come out. To
build this, Ward pulled down the house of
Thomas Dudley, the second governor of the
colony, kinsman, perhaps, of Leicester and
Amy Robsart. I say perhaps, because I do
not know, nor does any one else.

Now I am not going to instruct you
about methods of travel. Who am I, to de-
cide between a Columbia and a Crescent, and
I dare say those boys and girls of yours will
all expect to take the wheel. As it is John
Eliot we are tracing along, you will do well
to go up Warren Street far enough to see the
Latin School which he founded, which is on
Kearsarge Avenue, a little off Warren Street.
We call it the best classical school in America,
and we are very proud that John Eliot is its
founder.

But do not " dilate " with the wrong emo-

tion because it is on Kearsarge Avenue. Do
not say "How fine it is to give an Indian
name to the street where is John Eliot's
school!" Kearsarge Avenue is so named,
very properly, for Admiral Winslow's ship, the
"Kearsarge." He fought that fine ship when
she sank the "Alabama," and his house was
in this street. Kearsarge was and is the name
of a mountain in New Hampshire. Ships,
by the way, should never be named from
mountains, which can not move, but rather
from rivers, which can. Andes is a bad
name for a ship, and Niagara is a good one.
Kearsarge is not an Indian name. The
hill in New Hampshire was the property
of one Hezekiah Sargent, familiarly called
"Kiah Sargent." This name, for short, became "Keah-sarge," and the mountain is so
named to this day, and the ship from the
mountain and the street from the ship. I
tell this to you, dear Polly the younger, because we will study John Eliot's Massachusetts language as we go, and I do not
want you to hunt for any impossible ety-

mologies of stray Indian words like "Kearsarge." *

While the children are on their wheels,
running down to Canton, which is only ten
miles or so away, your husband and you may
as well take the trolley to Jamaica Plain,
where are the Eliot schoolhouse and the
Eliot Club—names which show at least that
we Roxbury people know how to honor our

---

* I have said above what I believe to be true. But the sub-
ject is one of the sorest among New Hampshire antiquarians.
There are now two Mount Kearsarges in New Hampshire. One
is in Warner, in the southern part of the State, and has been
known by the name of Kearsarge for a long time. The other is
in North Conway, in the northern part of the State, and was
formerly named Pequawket. In my judgment, it ought to be
named Pequawket to this day; it is mentioned by that name in
the fine ballad of Lovell's Fight, one of the few New England
ballads. But somebody chose to name it Kearsarge within the
memory of living men.

When the ship was built, the Governor of New Hampshire
was asked to furnish the names of some mountains in New
Hampshire, for which it might be named. He asked his son to
select two or three names, and among the rest the son selected
the name Kearsarge. He sent his letter to Washington. At the
same time he sent to the library for one of the early maps, on
which the Kearsarge in Warner, the original Kearsarge, was
named. Then and there he found that the hill was called
"Hezekiah Sargent's Hill." This gentleman told me, and I
have not chosen to go behind his information in the information which I have given to Polly Ingham.—EDWARD E. HALE.

ancestors, for Jamaica Plain is part of Roxbury. If anybody cares, the Jamaica planters
used to build their summer homes here before
the Revolution. Here you will take the train
for Canton, from our wonderful new station
house. And, once for all, the young people
and you had better invest fifteen cents at
Mr. Backup's for a Trolley Guide, and you
had better have in your pocket the little
book "By Broomstick Train." Then I shall
not have to be telling you at every second
line what these little books will tell you
much better.

Also, you may as well spend the waiting
minutes and hours of the pilgrimage by pick-
ing up the rudiments of the language to which
dear John Eliot gave so much of his life. It
is indeed rather strange that we know so little of it as we do. Richard Greenough was
in State Street one day, when a man asked
him what was the old name of Boston. "Tri-
mountain, do you mean?" asked Greenough.
"No—that would not answer." "Shawmut,
perhaps?" "Ah, yes, sir. Thank you. Now

you can tell me where the Shawmut Bank
is?"

Shawmut Avenue ends where Ward's battery stood. And you may as well remember
that "ut" or "et" means "the place," and is
here as a location after Mishawm, which
means "boats." Thus the peninsula was
named "the place of boats," not a bad name
for yachtsmen to remember now.

I do not "seem to remember," as our fine
vernacular has it, any other Indian names in
Boston but "Winnisimmet" for the ferry,
"Waban," "Monadnock," and "Waumbeck"
streets, and the village of "Mattapan." The
historian of Chelsea does not tell us the
meaning of Winnisimmet. I am disposed to
think that it is a euphonism for Winnesip-
pet. "Winne" is "fine," which we have in
"Winnepesaukee," "Winnipeg," and other
Algonkin words; "sippe" is "running water,"
and "et," like "ut," "the place." "The fine
place of running water" is a good name for
the mouth of Charles River. We have
"sippi" in Mississippi, "the great river"—a

name, by the way, which shows that Algon-
kins had to do with the naming of it. Some
of us think that when La Salle took Massachusetts Indians to make his discovery of that
river for him, he did so because they had been
there before. Coxe says so distinctly in his
"Carolana." But we can not really prove it.

Waban Street is named from the chief
Waban, who heard Eliot's first sermon. As
Dr. De Normandie tells us, his name meant
"the wind." Monadnock is named from the
distant mountain in New Hampshire. I suppose the word meant, originally, the "land of
wolves," or the "place of wolves."

At Canton station we shall wait for the
bicycles. Here we shall go to see the Eliot
Fountain at Ponkapog. There is a picture
of it in Dr. De Normandie's article. This is
the inscription: "In Memory of the Labors
of the Apostle Eliot among the Indians of
Ponkapog, 1655–1690."

Do you not wish that people would not
speak of the "labors" of a man whose
"work" they mean to praise? Paul spoke

of his own "labors," but this was in his modest way, because he must not praise himself. Work is the power of spirit over matter. Labor is drudgery, which wears out and wears down. A locomotive engineer says an engine "works well," or "she labors badly." He never would say she "labors well," or that she "works badly." This monument really marks the "work" of John Eliot.

I have brought you here because here you are so close to the Blue Hills which give the name to the State. "Massa" is "great"; it is of the same root as "Missi" in Mississippi; "wadtchu" is "hill," as in "Wachuset," and "et," as before said, is the terminal for "place." When you read in Eliot's Bible of the "Sermon on the Mount," you will read that Jesus sat on "wadtchu," "a mountain." I think it is rather pleasant that we have this connection with the name of the State.

You had better by all means go to Ponkapog pond, which gave the name to these Indians, if you have time. "Pog" or "Paug," as a termination, always means "inclosed water." I do not know—and they on the spot can tell you better than I—but I suppose that Ponkapog means "pond with a house," and I think there must have been a "hot-house" for the Turkish bath, as the Indians practiced. We have a Hot-house

The Eliot memorial at Newton.

Pond, thus named, within a mile of my house in the Narragansett country.

There would be a pretty ride, northwest for some fifteen miles across the country, to Natick, associated in everybody's mind with John Eliot. But we want to stop at Nonantum, the first place where he preached to them, so we will go back, bikes and all, to

Boston and take the steam train to Newton, or the pretty trolley road, with care about transfers. Look again in Dr. De Normandie's article for precise directions, or ask at the station in Newton. The place was on a hillside, perhaps half a mile from the station, and is now marked by an elaborate memorial, built by the Newton people.

"Here At Nonantum, Oct. 28, 1646, In
Waban's Wigwam
Near This Spot, JOHN ELIOT Began to
Preach The Gospel to
The Indians. Here He Founded The First
Christian
Community Of Indians Within The English Colonies."

This is the inscription.

Word had been given to the redskins that he would preach, and a large number of them met in Waban's wigwam. Eliot preached from Ezekiel xxxvii, 9: "Son of Man, say to the wind, Thus saith the Lord God." Now, as I said, "Waban" means wind, and the Indian braves who could understand thought that Eliot brought a direct message

from the Lord to Waban. Eliot says that
he had never thought of this in selecting the
text. But, of course, when it came to utter-
ing it, he must have seen how fortunate was

The old elm on Boston Common as it was.
From an old print.

the double meaning. Alas, that so much of
such preaching seems to have been talk to
the wind indeed!

Four years after, Natick—which they say
means "a place of hills," by abbreviation, I
think, from some longer word—was chosen
for a Christian settlement. The village is
not where the Natick of the railway stands.
That town, a large manufacturing place, is

6

about two miles from our Natick, which is the South Natick of the map, a pretty country village about two miles southeast from the railway station. Here you will find courteous and intelligent gentlemen and ladies who will be glad to show you the interesting memorials. First of all the John Eliot oak. Then the gravestone with the name of one of the converts, and indeed all the burial ground, is interesting. You had better take Old-Town Folks with you and look up the memories of Mrs. Stowe's work. Her husband, the distinguished Old Testament scholar, had the Scotch gift of second sight. He was born in Natick. He told me that when he was a child, looking northward over the comparatively level country over which you have ridden from Boston, he saw of a sudden a carriage without horses dragging a train of others behind it rush across the field from east to west. He told his story at home, and I think was whipped for lying. The line of carriages ran where you rode in one as you came to Natick! He

The Eliot Oak at Natick.

was a child, and even Stephenson had never dreamed of a railway train.

Mr. Stowe used to say that in his boyhood the Natick Indians had special privileges in his grandfather's house there. Any Indian might come in at any time and might sleep by the kitchen fire. A hogshead of cider was always set apart for the free use of any Indian. They were regarded as quite a different sort of being from the other tramps of the day, and had privileges of their own.

Polly dear—young Polly, I mean—see how far we have advanced in our study of the Massachusetts language. In twenty days of such study you would know more of it than my courier in Spain knew of the language of Sancho Panza. We have learned that "auke" or "ocke," means earth, place; "paug" or "pog" means inclosed water; "massa" means large; "missi" means large; "mishawm" means boats; "monad'n" means wolves; "nonantum" means rejoicing; "Natick" means place of hills; "pouka" means a hut or huts; "sippi" means river; "ut"

means at the place; "wadtchu" means hill;
"winne" means fine; and we knew before
that "wigwam" meant house.

For to-night's reading you may take a
few verses from Roger Williams:

> Coarse bread and water's most their fare.
>   O England's diet fine,
> Thy cup runs o'er with plenteous store
>   Of wholesome beer and wine.
>
> Sometimes God gives them fish or flesh,
>   Yet they're content without;
> And what comes in they part to friends
>   And strangers round about.
>
> God's providence is rich to his,
>   Let none distrustful be;
> In wilderness, in great distress,
>   These ravens have fed me.

> God gives them sleep on ground, on straw,
>   On sedgy mats, or board:
> When England's softest beds of down
>   Sometimes no sleep afford.
>
> I have known them leave their house or mat
>   To lodge a friend or stranger,
> When Jews and Christians oft have sent
>   Christ Jesus to the manger.

IV

TO FIND ONE'S WAY.

THE joke with strangers in Boston, who want to find their way without a map, is to say—

"Be sure what is the direction by compass of the place you are going to, and take the first street car which goes the opposite way."

This rule often answers very well. It might be expected in a town laid out by seafaring men, who often have to tack northeast and northwest if they want to go northward.

A better rule is that which Dr. Arnold gives somewhere in his letters, and which Stanley, the beloved Dean of Westminster, repeated to me when he was traveling in this country. When he came to Boston in 1878 I asked him what he wanted to see in Boston: did he want to see institutions, or

buildings, or men? for that he should see
whatever he wanted. He answered, good-
naturedly and with a laugh, that the old
historical impulse had broken out again. "I
want to see anything about history. Show
me where the Old Elm was on Boston Common. I know that it has been blown down,
but I want to see what there is left of it."
He told me that the first day he arrived he
had gone to the top of the State House. He
said this was in following out a rule of the
great Thomas Arnold, who said that when
you visited a new place you ought to see it
from above, that you might understand afterward something of its geography. And
afterward Phillips Brooks gave me a most
amusing account of this visit to the top of
the State House. Stanley was a little man,
light and active; and Brooks said he ran up
the stairways of the State House as a spar-
row might do, in advance, while poor Brooks,
who must have weighed two hundred and
twenty-five pounds if he weighed an ounce,
was toiling slowly behind.

I took Stanley at his word. It was in the ride we took then that I showed him Eliot's grave. We took a carriage at once, quite early in the afternoon, and went first that he might see where the Wishing Stone was, and so down to the iron fence which surrounds the relics of the Old Elm. It is now twenty years since the greater part of that tree was blown down, but quite a re-spectable "scyon" is growing up from the roots, and our great grandchildren will say that from that tree Mary Dyer was hanged. We went up Highland Street, stopped at my own house, and then went to what there was left of Ward's old fort on Fort Hill Street. Observe, this is not the "Fort Hill" of the original Trimount, but was named Fort Hill because Ward put his fort here. It is Gen-eral Ward's large fort, sometimes called in the braggart authors "a place of arms." If you read the account of it which Hilliard d'Auberteuil, a Frenchman, published in Paris in 1779 you would say it was another Gibraltar.

I have always supposed that Ward made the fort for the sake of giving his soldiers something to do. It was quite large; it had four bastions, one at each corner, and it absolutely commanded the passage out by the Neck. No English force could have moved across the Neck while the Americans held that fort. The small fort, where the Universalist church stood till lately, and where a row of small shops has just now been built, is that we saw the John Eliot day.

I remember that as we stood on this hill and looked around, Stanley asked me which was the forest into which Hester fled with her child in Hawthorne's book. I showed him the edge of the Blue Hills, and told him I thought she probably went there. Afterward we saw Warren's birthplace; we went to Meeting-house Hill that he might get the view from the high land there. I remember he was delighted to find the word "meeting-house" in familiar use, as the carriage driver himself used it in speaking to me. We followed the course by which Ward and Thomas led the American troops on the night of the 4th of March, and I showed him what there is left of the old fortifications on the South Boston hills. So we returned, after the gas lights were lighted, to the Brunswick House, where he was staying.

I give these details because that very course, in a carriage or on bicycles, is a good route for any one to follow who has but a few hours for history, besides that which we have already studied. You will see from the South Boston hills Hog Island, where Putnam won his first laurels in the Revolution. You can see the two rivers, the Mystic and the Charles, and Bunker Hill between them. You can see how the American army hemmed in the British force, commanded first by Gage and afterward by Howe.

The traveler ought to observe, wherever he goes in Boston, that the very names of the streets carry him back through the history of the town. We should not repeat those names of streets as if there were no meaning attached to them. When we say "Hanover

Street," we should remember what it was to these good people that the house of Hanover came to the throne, and that the Stuarts, whom they hated so thoroughly, were driven away forever. We should remember, and we should thank God, that there is no Stuart Street, no Bourbon Street, and no Hapsburg Street.

When a visitor from abroad goes through Newbury Street, we do not want him to think merely that the houses are all nailed up, and that all his friends have moved to Bar Harbor or Magnolia or Swampscott. This will be true if he arrives between the first of June and the first of October; but let him, as he turns away discouraged, recollect how Charles I and Prince Rupert turned the tails of their horses on Newbury in England, and retired before a certain Oliver Cromwell and his troopers. Let him say to himself, "These old Puritans named Newbury Street that their children might remember some such passages as that in history." This Newbury Street is not the Newbury

Street they so named; they had occasion afterward to change the name of that street to Washington Street, in honor of a certain George Washington who followed in the footsteps of that Oliver Cromwell.

When the stranger goes through Marlborough Street, looking for some few of his cousins who may not have gone to their summer bathing place, let him remember how, when the great Duke of Marlborough was beating the French and certain allies of theirs, we were rejoicing here and having Thanksgiving Days in his honor, and that a part of our Washington Street was named Marlborough Street at that time. If he come up from his train by Beach Street, let him remember that here was a beach, and that adventurous boys pushed off their dories as they went out to fish. If he come through Federal Street, let him remember that here was a meeting house made famous by one William Ellery Channing in after years. And the street changed its name from Long Lane on the famous day when

Convention did in State House meet,
And when it wouldn't hold 'em
They all went down to Federal Street,
And there the truth was told 'em.

That is to say, it was in this meeting house
that the convention sat which adopted the
Federal Constitution.

So, as history goes by, it has left its im-
prints. And that is a dull master of a Boston school who can not illustrate the two
hundred and fifty years which have passed,
in the daily walks of his pupils. I was very
much honored, some years ago, when some
kindergarten children, none of whom, I think,
were more than seven years old, gave me
a set of their own drawings of the history
of Boston from the time that Winthrop
shook hands with Massasoit down to the time
when the "Constitution," built at the North
End, fought "bold Dacres." I suppose they
will name the new park at the North End
"Constitution Park" in honor of Hart's
Yard, where her keel was laid and where
she sprang into life as a thing of beauty.

We have no Constitution Street nor Place
nor Wharf nor Park at this moment, but
we will have soon. The people at that
time observed that the "Constitution" and
the "United States" won all the victories,
while the "President" was captured and the
"Congress" was blockaded.

Some names commemorate events which
would else be wholly forgotten. When General Eaton took the city of Derne in northern Africa, by taking the responsibility of a
military movement which no one had ordered,
Mr. Samuel Russell, then a young man,
thought that sufficient deference was not paid
Eaton, and himself had a sign painted with
the name "Derne Street" upon it, which he
nailed upon the corner of the street on which
now the northern entrances of the State
House open. The State House Park of to-
day is therefore bounded by Beacon Street,
which commemorates days as early as when
the colony defied Charles I; by Derne Street,
which commemorates a victory which everybody has forgotten; Bowdoin Street, which

commemorates the first name on the list of the State's delegates to the Continental Congress; and Hancock Avenue, which bears the name of the first signer of the Declaration of Independence. When we "get round to it," as a New England phrase says, we shall erect a statue in his memory.

Any one of my age in America has known personally people who had an active part in the Revolution and has seen many physical memorials of the Revolution in Boston which have not been preserved till today. When I was a boy, for instance, the square redoubt which General Gage's troops threw up on Boston Common was in a better condition for its purpose than it was the day after it was built, for it was well sodded by the grass of more than fifty years which had grown on it. In winter we dragged our sleds up through what would be called, I suppose, a sally port, and we coasted down through the same as far as Charles Street Mall, which was then new. Some "capability man" or incapable improver has since

smoothed off the breastworks, because when
it rained, water stood behind them.

When, by the direction of the formidable
batteries on Dorchester Heights, Washington drove the English out from the town,
General Howe took his whole army to Halifax. With the army went a very considerable number of the Tories of Boston and
Massachusetts. Washington had no objec-
tion to permitting any Tories who wished to
go into the besieged city and help General
Howe eat the salt pork and salt beef which
he had provided for the besieged. I have
never seen in print a little scrap which was
traditional when I was a boy:

And what have you got for all your designing
But a town without dinner to sit down and dine in?

A good many such scraps still lingered
among people as old as I am, whose ancestry
spent the months of siege inside. I have
myself seen a lady who was at Faneuil Hall,
as a girl of fifteen, when Burgoyne's play,
The Blockade of Boston, which was being

7

acted by English officers, was broken up by the news of a sudden attack which Putnam had made upon their barracks in Charlestown. The girls had to go home that night without their escorts. The gay officers were ordered to their posts.

The Tory wits of the town for years before had had their share in making ballads, as our wits had done.

That patriot Jimmy Otis, that bully in disguise,
That well-known tyke of Yorkshire, that magazine
  of lies:
And he will mount the rostrum, and loudly he will
  bray,
" Rebel, rebel, rebel, rebel, rebel, America!"

This is one of such verses. It is to the air of the British Grenadiers, which is still a favorite in English mess-rooms. I crossed the ocean in 1859 with some English army officers, who sang to us the modern version, which brought in the name of Lord Raglan and the battles of Inkermann and the Alma. I was able to give them the verses of 1775, then nearly eighty years old and unknown to them before.

Come, come, fill up your glasses, and drink a health
  to those
Who carry caps and pouches, and wear their loopéd
  clothes.
For be you Whig or Tory or any mortal thing,
Be sure that you give glory to George our gracious
  king.
For if you prove rebellious, we'll thunder in your
  ears
Huzza, huzza, huzza, huzza, for the British Grenadiers!

I may say in passing that the ballad, now
so well known, of "Father 'n' I went down
to Camp," by Edward Bangs, which belongs
to nearly the same time, was written on the
other side of the line.

Among the refugee merchants who put
all their available stores on board their own
vessels to go to Halifax under the escort of
General Howe, was my own grandmother's
grandfather, a timid merchant at the North
End, and, as I believe, a highly respectable
person. I am a little apt to think that he
signed all the petitions and remonstrances
which were offered him by the leaders on
either side. He seems to have had a catholic

indifference of opinion, but he was so quiet a
person that he had not removed the family
out of town during the siege.

Unfortunately for all concerned, except
Washington and his army, the fleet in the
bay experienced very rough weather before
Howe and his admirals were ready to make
the voyage to Halifax. My great-great-grandfather's wife was so seasick that she declared
she could not survive the voyage; and fortunately for me and mine the sloop on which
they were all engaged ran into the harbor
of Newburyport. To this fortunate *mal de
mer* of my great-great-grandmother do I owe
it that, so far as she is concerned, I am an
American citizen, or, indeed, I might say,
that I am anybody anywhere. I have told in
another place the story of the mutton broth
which she received in the siege. At the
time, the present of the shoulder of mutton
from which it was made was ascribed, I believe, to miracle. In the last dozen years we
have learned that it came from Major Mon-
crief as a present to Doctor Eliot, and Doctor

Eliot left it, before light, at the back door of the house in which the invalid was lying. This is, I believe, the Doctor Eliot of whom it is said that, in his broad catholicity, one Sunday when he was engaged in praying for all sorts and conditions of men, for the sick, the prisoners, the sailors, the strangers within our gates, and so on, he concluded this petition by the generous wish, "Last of all, O Lord, for the poor old Devil himself, that his sufferings may be somewhat mitigated." I can not, of course, vouch for the absolute truth of the anecdote; I do know that it reflects very well the large generosity of the man.

I have often seen Major Melvill pass our house, the same who has been immortalized by Doctor Holmes in the ballad of The Last Leaf. He wrote this at about the time when I used to see the old gentleman, in his cocked hat, his blue coat, and his buff breeches, pass up or down School Street, by the house where we then lived. He was called, truly or not, one of the survivors of the Tea Party.

With regard to those survivors, there is
an interesting fact to be borne in mind,
which is, indeed, an illustration of the credit
to be given to many historical traditions.
The proper Tea Party—that is to say, the
body of men who combined and went together to Griffin's Wharf to throw the tea
into the sea—organized itself in a Masonic
lodge, or in Masonic lodges, and the members
took an oath that they would never reveal
the events of that night. To this oath they
all held themselves bound till the last one of
them died. The enterprise required that
the North End section should pass the Old
South Meeting-House, where a meeting was
going forward, adjourned from Faneuil Hall,
to consider the whole business of the tea.
This meeting was not strictly a Boston town
meeting, although the Boston town meeting
was merged in it; but there were citizens
from all the neighboring towns present. At
the moment when the disguised Mohawks
came to the meeting-house, Sam Adams, who
was presiding, said, "This meeting can do

The Frog Pond, Boston Common.

nothing more to save the country," and adjourned it. All the three or four thousand people who were present then followed " the Mohawks" to the wharf. By this time, undoubtedly, all Boston knew what was going on, and as the sun went down and as the moon came out on the scene, it may be fairly guessed that nineteen twentieths of the adult male population of Boston was on the slope of Fort Hill or on the shore, rendering such assistance as they could in the enterprise in hand. But one tradition and another tell how, when new men attempted to board the ships, they were prevented by sentries established by the original conspirators. These conspirators were men who understood all about unloading ships; it was the business of many of them in daily life; and the cargoes were withdrawn with haste and the three hundred and seventy-three chests of tea were emptied into the sea. Then everybody went home. The tea, in enormous masses, drifted up and down the harbor on the surface of the water for days; a good deal of it

was left on South Boston Point. From these
sources and from the boots of the men who
were at work, come the specimens of the tea
which are shown in almost all the museums
of New England to this day.

It will be observed, then, that almost
every adult citizen of Boston was engaged,
more or less directly, in throwing the tea
overboard. A small number of these persons,
perhaps a hundred more or less, had sworn
never to mention that fact. So far as anybody knows, they never did mention it. Of
which this curious consequence has come into
history, that if, within the last seventy-five
years, any old gentleman has said that he was
of the Boston Tea Party, it is perfectly sure
that he was *not* one of the party of men
who really did throw the tea into the harbor.
If, on the other hand, any nice old gentleman, asked by his grandchildren if he were
of the Tea Party, smiled and put off the sub-
ject and began talking about General Washington or General Gage, it is well-nigh certain that he was one of that confederation.

In other words, the men who said they threw
the tea overboard did not, and the men who
did not say they did, were the parties most
engaged.

As for personal intimacy with the people
who fought in the war, I can say but little.
A little boy of five did not dare run up to
Major Melvill and ask him to tell stories of
the Revolution. I have, however, with these
eyes, seen the banners which Stark sent down
from Bennington, as his tribute of gratitude
to the Massachusetts militia. Alas for the
sentiment of such things! Mr. Kuhn, then
the messenger, as he was called, of the Legis-
lature—holding the same duties as those now
discharged by the sergeant-at-arms—found
that the banners were dirty and moth-eaten,
and put them into the dust-barrel one fine
day; so that they have ceased to exist for
mortal eyes for the last sixty years. People
of the same make-up wanted last year to do
the same thing with the State House itself,
but have fortunately been foiled.

The excellent story of the Boston school-

boys who waited upon the English general is
well known to most children in the Northern
States. I had that story told me by one of
the survivors of the committee appointed by
the Boston Latin School to attend to this
affair. His name was Jonathan Darby Robins,
and in the year 1846 he was still living, with
a perfectly fresh memory of this transaction,
which had taken place not long before the
battle of Lexington. The Latin School then
stood where Parker's hotel is now, on the
south side of that School Street to which the
school gave its name. The spot is directly
opposite where Franklin's statue now stands.
This is just where it should be, for Franklin
was a schoolboy in the same school, when the
schoolhouse occupied its present site where
the statue now is. The boys, before and
after school, were in the habit of coasting
from the hill, then higher than it is now,
which rises above the Congregational House,
behind the great pile of the new Tremont
Buildings. They coasted down what we call
Beacon Street across Tremont Street, and

kept on down School Street to Washington
Street. General Haldimand, a brigadier in
the English army, occupied the house which
stood on School Street, next below where the
Parker House now is. Haldimand's servant
did not like this coasting business, and he
scattered ashes on the coast so as to make it
easier for his master and the officers to come
in and out at the Beacon Street door. Finding that their remonstrances failed, the Latin
School boys appointed a committee of their
first class to wait upon Haldimand. Haldimand received them courteously, and the boys
told him that coasting was one of their in-
alienable rights. Haldimand did not wish to
make more trouble in a town which was as
ripe for rebellion as Boston, so he sent for the
servant and gave him a good scolding, and
bade him take care, every cold night, to repair
the coast by pouring water upon it, which
should freeze so that it should be kept in
good condition for the boys.

With the vagueness of another generation, the scene of this exploit has been trans-

ferred to Boston Common. No Boston boy then thought any more of going out to coast on the Common than he would now think of going down to coast on Deer Island. The painters have represented the visit also as made at the Province House; but in point of fact the visit, as Mr. Robins told me himself, was made on Haldimand at his own quarters.

BOSTON.

The rocky nook with hilltops three
  Looked eastward from the farms,
And twice each day the flowing sea
  Took Boston in its arms;
The men of yore were stout and poor,
And sailed for bread to every shore.

And where they went on trade intent
  They did what freemen can,
Their dauntless ways did all men praise,
  The merchant was a man.
The world was made for honest trade,
To plant and eat be none afraid.

   .   .   .   .   .   .

The wild rose and the barberry thorn
  Hung out their summer pride,
Where now on heated pavements worn
  The feet of millions stride.

Fair rose the planted hills behind
  The good town on the bay,
And where the western hills declined
  The prairie stretched away.

What care though rival cities soar
  Along the stormy coast,
Penn's town, New York, and Baltimore,
  If Boston knew the most!

They laughed to know the world so wide;
  The mountains said "Good-day!
We greet you well, you Saxon men,
  Up with your towns, and stay!"
The world was made for honest trade,
To plant and eat be none afraid.

" For you," they said, " no barriers be,
  For you no sluggard rest;
Each street leads downward to the sea,
  Or landward to the west."

O happy town beside the sea,
  Whose roads lead everywhere to all;
Than thine no deeper moat can be,
  No stouter fence, no steeper wall!

    .   .   .   .   .   .

The sea, returning day by day,
  Restores the world-wide mart;
So let each dweller on the bay
  Fold Boston in his heart,
Till these echoes be choked with snows,
Or over the town blue ocean flows.

Let the blood of her hundred thousands
　　Throb in each manly vein ;
And the wits of all her wisest
　　Make sunshine in her brain.
For you can teach the lightning speech,
And round the globe your voices reach.

And each shall care for other,
　　And each to each shall bend,
To the poor a noble brother,
　　To the good an equal friend.

A blessing through the ages thus
　　Shield all thy roofs and towers !
GOD WITH THE FATHERS, SO WITH US,
　　Thou darling town of ours !

V.

HARVARD COLLEGE.

YES, my dear young ladies, I understand
all you say. There will not be time, perhaps,
for you to go to see Emerson's home, and Dr.
Channing's house, and Mr. Prescott's, which
is torn down, and Mr. Bancroft's, which is
burned down. But why not go to the college
itself, where they were matured, and " dilate
with the right emotions " there? "Might
not one see, indeed, at the same time, Mr.
Fiske's home, and Mr. Eliot's, and Mrs. Alice
Freeman Palmer's, and Dr. Everett's, and
Mr. Shaler's, if only from the outside ? "

Certainly; yes, dear girls, all things are
possible to the brave and to the elect. And
all these shall you see in one excursion.

Two years ago I had been lecturing on
The Human Washington, in Philadelphia,

and as I returned to my home there, one of
my audience joined me in the car to ask me
if I was personally acquainted with President
Washington. As this remark showed me that
she thought me at least one hundred and
fifteen years old, I was well pleased that, as
we Yankees have it, she thought I "bore my
years so well." Mr. James T. Fields had a
better story than mine. He had been reading
at Cambridge his charming lecture on John
Dryden, and a law student, who had been
specially interested, asked him if he knew
Dryden personally. This implied that Mr.
Fields's flowing, black hair had stood well
the winters of nearly two centuries. These
anecdotes I mention because we are now
going to Cambridge, where we oldsters speak
always as if we had, with these very hands
and heads of ours, done the whole thing, or
with these very eyes seen it done. Thus, "we
printed Eliot's Bible here," means that Harvard College did it, and so we did it our-
selves. She is our Alma Mater, and when
we were in the loins of our ancestors Har-

vard College did this thing of which we
speak.

Yes, my dear Mrs. Ingham, an open street
car it shall be. I am not sure that they ride
in them in Paradise; but a charming Boston
day, wind from the bay, thermometer at 68°
rising, you and I will find it hard to take a
more agreeable vehicle. "Please stop at
Wadsworth." To you aside, dear Polly, now
the man has gone forward, I will whisper
that this is an old conductor. He is the very
man who "took a day off" because there was
a new volume of Browning which he wanted
to read. All the drivers and all the other
conductors heard of this, and so they all took
a day or two off to read Browning, and this
was the way that the great strike of ten
years ago began. So at least they tell that
story on us in Chicago.

But before we come to Harvard Square,
where "Wadsworth" is, observe that we rise
and fall a little. We ascend and descend
the side of Dana Hill. On our left here used
to be some redoubts thrown up to keep the

English from invading Cambridge by way of Charles River.

As late as the end of the last century— say in 1790, or thereabouts—this very Dana Hill was offered to the college, it is said, for only five thousand dollars. Alas and alas— there were no five thousand dollars! President Eliot would find it easier to-day to collect five million dollars for the college than it would have been then to collect five thousand. If, by good fortune, some angel in heaven had dropped a gold nugget worth five thousand dollars—say a hundred and fifty ounces of gold (less than ten pounds)— and if the president had picked it up, and had bought Dana Farm—why, the college to-day would have a home as large as any of her Western sisters.

But this was not to be. So you see "the yard," as we call it—never "the campus "—is not so big as it would be in Nebraska.

Here is Wadsworth, and here the Browning-loving conductor drops us. The dear old house is nearly two centuries old; and you

Wadsworth House, Cambridge.

and I, Mrs. Ingham, may be glad if we ever live in a better. The government of the college, which was then really the State government, wanted the minister of the First Church in Boston for president of the college. But he would not go to Cambridge unless they would build him a fit home. So they built this home for him. It is a good type of the architecture of 1700. You see it has the comfortable and convenient gambrel roof of that time.

I met a lady yesterday who told me she had read with interest of the life and work of Monsieur Mansard, the French architect, and she asked where she should find the life of Monsieur Gambrel. For our purposes his is a better roof, not to say more picturesque, than the French Mansard. See this fine old balustrade to the stairways. And what paneling they had! This handsome parlor on the left is the "ministers' room." Here, every day, in term time, from nine to twelve, the minister "in residence" sits—writes to his wife, perhaps, in far Duluth, or wherever you please,

unless one of his undergraduate boys comes
in on a visit of courtesy, of loneliness, or of
inquiry. Trust me, who know, there are no
three hours in that minister's life more interesting than those he thus spends here, with
the frank sympathy of intercourse with these
fine young fellows. "Dr. Primrose, we are
going to wear hunting shirts in the procession. We fellows did not know whether the
fringes should be yellow or purple. What
do you think?" Or, perhaps, more seriously,
"Dr. Primrose, you said in chapel that thus
and thus. . . ." "Do you think the Saviour
meant . . . ?" and so on, in the gravest and
dearest intimacies of life. Or, "Dr. Primrose, please read this letter. Do you think I
ought to . . . ?" and so on in a young man's
frank confidence.

Here are some autographs you will like
to see in the memorandum book of the
preachers. There is Dr. Vincent's ; here is
Phillips Brooks's. This is the picture of old
Wadsworth. Yes, Longfellow's great grandfather, or some sort of a cousin. But one

must not stay here. Indeed, I could not, of course, have brought you in were we not in vacation. Perhaps I should have explained that at Harvard there are six chaplains representing different religious communions. For three weeks at a time one of these gentlemen is "in residence" here to serve the students in any way he can.

Come out of this side door. When this was the president's house, in Kirkland's day, this office was built for him. You never heard of Kirkland, Polly, but you have heard of his "freshman," the boy who ran his errands for him. His name it was Ralph Waldo Emerson, and his room was over the office, up there. One of these days, "when we get round to it," we are going to put a bronze plate here to say so.

Things were not so grand in those days in the young fellows' rooms as you will see them to-day, Miss Polly.

It is rather less than a century since the little school of the fathers began to take on the style of a college. The era of the deter-

mination that it should be elevated from the
somewhat wooden arrangements of a poor
school into an institution where young men
could really be trained for the duties of men
may be roughly marked by the inauguration
of John Thornton Kirkland as president of
the college. Kirkland was an accomplished
scholar. He had the advantages of life in
the excellent social circles of the Boston of
his time. The appointment of Dr. Kirkland
marked a determination that the college should
lead in the higher education of America.

That is to say, the rich men of Boston determined to have a place worthy of the new
nation where their sons could be educated.
Enough of these gentlemen knew what such
an education was, and they were willing to
give the money which should elevate this
school to a higher plane. With the enlargement of its resources, and with the character
of the men who were teachers, everything
changed. Little details as to the manner of
life changed also, and gradually, between the
year 1800 and our year 1898, the whole ex-

The College Yard.

ternal method of life has changed at Cambridge. I was in college between the years
1835 and 1839, when this change was already
in progress, but before the college had at-
tained the conditions of to-day. For a little
instance, which is a convenient one, I remember that most of my older friends were
surprised when they were told that I was to
have a carpet in my room. To the minds of
people who had not known what college life
was within the ten years before, a carpet was
entirely out of place in a college room. I
am quite sure that there was not a pianoforte
in any undergraduate's room. And a curious
illustration of life elsewhere appeared one
day when Mr. Lovering in lecturing spoke
of billiard balls and their movement on the
table. More than half of the members of
my class had never seen a billiard ball. Dr.
Peabody has given some details of the last
experiences of the " Buttery." This was the
place to which students went for a mug of
milk, some rolls of bread, and a piece of but-
ter, from which the breakfast and the supper

of the undergraduate was made, in his own
room. The Buttery was a shed at the east
end of Harvard Hall. Till lately some trace
of its roof could be seen on the eastern wall
of that building. But now they are covered
by Ampelopsis. At commons, that is, in Dr.
Peabody's day, and in the days of the older
graduates whom I knew best, no meal was
served excepting dinner. A like simplicity
prevailed in many other matters, the forms
of which in some cases were borrowed from
the methods of the English colleges and in
some from those of a log-cabin.

On the other hand, there were some traditions of academic life which would be considered now formal or quaint. No person could
appear in a recitation room or at chapel who
was not dressed in black, or in what was
called "black mixed" in the regulations.
This rule was quite strictly enforced in the
earlier part of my college life, but we emerged
from it so far that in 1838 and 1839 there
came in a fashion in summer of wearing hunting shirts of every conceivable color; and

these were permitted by what we called the parietal board, the board which managed such details.

The visitor will do almost as well on foot for the Cambridge excursions which are to be described as on wheels. But, of course, an open carriage with an intelligent "driver" is a convenience. First, the library—Gore Hall. The original building is a reduced copy in granite of one of the chapels in the English Cambridge. Perhaps, one day, when we have built a larger library, we may use this as a chapel. But we enter on one side of this; this library is open, thank Heaven! every day in the year. Attentive and trained assistants will do the honors, and you may spend days here happily. Be sure to see the mask of Cromwell's face, the original MS. of Longfellow's Excelsior, and ask for any American map, or indeed for anything else in history which interests you, and you will be apt to see it. For this century they have the original of the prize papers of every man who ever graduated here—say, Emerson's, Sumner's, Phillips's, Parkman's, and so on.

But if you only have one hour we must go on. "Mr. Kiernan, this lady would like to see the Logia which they dug up in Egypt. Will it trouble you to show it to her?"

"Certainly not. Here is the facsimile. Or would you like to see the Sinaitic MS. in facsimile?"

"No; we must not wait. Thank you, Mr. Kiernan, we must go on."

These people whom you see in summer in the great reading room in Gore Hall, and these who walk about in the yard as if they were visitors—as we are—asking which was Henry Knox's room, and where Chickataw- but lived, these are not Harvard students proper, nor "annex" or Radcliffe girls. These are in the "summer schools," and to most of them the college yard at Harvard is as new as it is to you. Why, yes! Surely this is Hollis Holworthy! My dear fellow, how are you? I have not seen you since you re-

The College Library.

9

ceived your diploma, *magna cum laude!*
Twenty-five years ago! Is it possible? and
this fine fellow? Really? Seventeen years
old, is he? And you are looking at carpets
for his room in the fall? Now you ladies are
safe. Mr. Holworthy shall take Miss Ingham
to see the Vas-Sol* and the statue of Day,
the printer, while I and Mrs. Ingham——"
" No? Then we will all keep together, only
we have but three hours left, and I shall
hurry you everywhere. Miss Ingham, this
is Mr. Holden Holworthy. He is an undergraduate here, and will explain everything to
you. Yes, you will, Holden; a fellow who
has only just passed his examinations knows
more than anybody else in the world."

So we cross to the old building with the
cupola and the bell. Yonder, up four stories,
is the narrow gulf which Tutor McKean
jumped over in his undergraduate days. He
had been melting pewter into the college

---

* The Vas-Sol tombstone is in the burying ground opposite
the college yard. It is the same stone which Mr. Lowell and
Dr. Holmes refer to. Vas-Sol—a vase, and the sun—represent
the Vassal family.

bell, heard steps below, walked down the
roof and sprang across the little gap to the
roof of Hollis, so as to secure his retreat.
A little triangle on the end wall, if you
could see it, would show where the Buttery
was when fellows breakfasted and supped in
their rooms. They came here for milk and
bread. At the head of these stone steps
there used to be a sundial a hundred years
ago. We have the dial now, rescued from an
old junk shop, and when "we get round to
it" we shall mount it here again. They need
another sundial on the gable of Massachusetts
yonder. At the pump yonder, Holden, your
grandfather filled his pail once a day or more
often, and then he lugged it up into the
fourth story of Hollis. Yes, there is the old
elm which we used to dance around on class
day. Holden, that little brick chapel is
named for the ladies whose honored name
you bear. They were rich Nonconformists
of England, who sent word that they should
like to build a chapel for the college. The
corporation was frugal—as it is now—

counted its little handful of students, I suppose, and allowed for a possible increase of
fifty per cent, and built this dear little sanc-
tuary. When the ladies Holden got the
bills, they were sadly disappointed because
it was so small. They had imagined something like the magnificent chapels of Oxford
or Cambridge. Such, at least, is the tradition.
That was my room, for two years, up one
flight, rear of Stoughton. Yes, named after
the old governor. But this is not the old
Stoughton. That was burned down in the
siege of Boston. Here is Holworthy—named
for your kinsman, Hollis ; and now I am going
to hurry you out from the "yard" proper
by the new gate because I want you to
have half an hour at Memorial Hall, half
an hour at each of the museums, and Holden there will want to take us all into the
gymnasium, and you must at least see the observatory and the Botanic Garden.

As we come out, dear Mrs. Ingham, pray
notice how characteristic and venerable this
fine gateway is. Really it is not ten years

old, but it looks a good two centuries already. No, Polly, dear, you can not go into the Fogg Museum to-day. There are pictures and prints and other fine art, but Mr. Holworthy must bring you for a whole afternoon there. Now we must cross the street to what people used to call the Delta, and here is the Memorial Hall.

Yes, Miss Polly, "Delta," as the triangular island at the mouth of the Nile is a delta. This roadway which we have crossed was once the Concord turnpike, and when they made it, it cut off this corner, and then the corner had the classical name given to it. When the gymnastic fad came in, say in the year 1827, under Lieber and Follen and Beck—German exiles of the days of the Holy Alliance—parallel bars and horses of wood for leaping, and great gallows trees for ladders and swings and climbing were placed here. Here is the place of which Freeman Clarke tells such awful stories of his climbing. All this apparatus went to its own place under the destructive influences of

those prehistoric times, and the Delta became
the ballground for prehistoric football and
baseball.

After the war, however, when we determined to build the Memorial Hall, Mr. Eliot
arranged for the great Jarvis playground,
and all the games went there so that this
hall might be built on the Delta ; and here is
Mr. French's fine statue of John Harvard.
See, Miss Ingham, how wistfully he looks
into the west. It was "the western mystery" which they all hoped to solve. And
he, instead of solving it, must die ! And he
knows he must die ! So he leaves the college
to work out the mystery for him. Hardly
thirty years old !

Come into the hall. Here is the real memorial hall, between the dining room and the
theater. Mr. Hollis, will you show the ladies
the inscriptions ? You do not remember the
men. I had rather not talk here.

And from this monumental transept
there opens the great hall of the college, pic-

ture gallery, and dining room, and on the
right, opposite to it, the Sanders Theater.
Yes, Mrs. Ingham, we can go into the dining
hall. If it was term time they would be set-
ting the tables. These marble busts are of
the presidents of the college for this century;
and the three Presidents we have given the
nation are here. Old John Adams there is
by Copley; his son is there, the head, I think,
is by Stuart ; and Hayes, in the middle there,
is by Chase. The windows have been given
as memorials by separate classes as they graduated. This is John Lovell, who caned John
Hancock when he did not know his Latin
grammar. Hancock himself is somewhere
yonder, I believe. Stay as long as you like ;
only there is so little time. We will cross
over to the theater.

Sanders Theater this is, named from the
Sanders whose money built it. It is well-
nigh perfect for its purpose; and all the high
functions are held here. On the Commence-
ment day when the fine statue of President
Josiah Quincy, by Story, was first displayed

here, his great grandson, the present Mayor of Boston, Josiah Quincy, was graduated. He had one of the leading parts, *magna cum laude;* and on the platform were seated two more Josiahs, his grandfather, who had been mayor as his father had been, and Mr. Josiah P. Quincy, every way worthy of his place in the line. The father of the President was the Josiah Quincy of the days before the Revolution.

But the Sanders half hour is up. Just come round to the western corridor and see the statues. Now we must cross to the Agassiz Museum. It is only a few steps; we may as well walk. We are in " Professors' Row," as old-fashioned people used to call it. Farther on it is the " Milk row " by which Percy and the rest fled to Charlestown on the night of the New England Chevy Chase.

We shall come in at the west door of the museum, because, if you ladies see nothing else, you must see the glass flowers. I will give you half an hour where you might spend

half a day. You can not see anything like
this collection anywhere else in the world.
The ladies of Professor Ware's family en-
abled the college to retain the services of the
maker of these glass flowers, and the experts
of his family, all of them in Europe, to make
this wonderful permanent exhibit of the
American flora. The colors will not fade, as
they do when flowers are pressed, and with
scientific precision every detail of each plant
is presented for study and for you and me to
see how beautiful the world is.

And have you seen the meteorites, Hol·
worthy? These have been placed here since
your time.

Botanists and other flower lovers will be
apt to linger, passing from case to case, till it
is time to close the hall; but if people are
resolute and can tear themselves away, they
may pass to the zoölogical sections, and just
take in an idea of the wonderful resources
which they offer to students. Louis Agassiz
is the founder of the museum. His son Alex·
ander has given to it its place and dignity in

The Johnston Gate, Harvard College.

the great collections of the world. The arrangement seems well-nigh perfect for students or for sightseers. For in this central room where we now are, are what I may call types or specimens of all the " kingdoms," as we used to say, of animal life. This room alone would be an admirable museum for any college. Beasts, birds, fishes, insects, everything which has animal life, all are represented here. And all the large halls which radiate from this hall are given to the subdivisions which are here indexed, if I may say so. Thus, here is a lion, and in the room for beasts of the cat tribe, if that is now their name, we shall find another lion; and yet again, in the hall for African beasts we shall find another lion. But, for an all-round view, we who are not specialists may well begin with the index room here. Indeed, indeed, we shall want more than a half hour.

Divide your time as you please, unknown friend whom I have been advising. I have

15612B

been leading you as I should like to be led. In that avenue on which the museum opens you will like to look in on Divinity Hall, and on the charming library and curious museum adjoining it. Whatever else you leave out, you must go into the separate Museum of American Archæology, fortunate if you find Professor Putnam there, and if he can give you even a few minutes ; and remember that we have left one museum unexplored in the college yard.

You have also left, unseen as yet, what is left of the Sanders playground and the soldiers' field ; and there is Longfellow's house, and Lowell's, where is to be Elmwood Park ; and Mount Auburn ; and, as I said, the observatory ; and, best of all, perhaps, the botanical garden.

Then you would like to see the Riverside printing house, and the old intrenchments in the Hovey gardens, and everything else in Cambridge ; but I am afraid that all this means that you must buy one of the nice Cambridge guides at the admirable bookshops, or wait, perhaps, till Mrs. Ingham and Miss Ingham and I meet there again.

So we will turn around and be thankful that there is so much for another visit. But no, dear Pauline, you shall not be disappointed. We will take our car higher up on Garden Street, and here is the statue of the first New England printer; and here is what papa promised you—the old elm beneath which Washington's commission was read, and where he took command of the army.

And to-night you shall sing every line of "Father 'n' I went down to Camp." Here was the camp. Some of the soldiers were in old Massachusetts, which we saw just now. As you ride in, Mr. Holworthy ought to be able to show some of the earthworks. And here is the dear old song which you shall sing to-night to the tune of Yankee Doodle. It was written by Edward Bangs :

> Father and I went down to camp
> Along with Captain Gooding,
> And there we see the men and boys
> As thick as hasty pudding.

And there we see a thousand men
  As rich as Squire David ;
And what they wasted every day,
  I wish it could be savéd.

The 'lasses they eat every day
  Would keep a house a winter ;
They have so much that, I'll be bound,
  They eat it when they're a mind to.

And there we see a swamping gun,
  Large as a log of maple,
Upon a deuced little cart,
  A load for father's cattle.

And every time they shoot it off
  It takes a horn of powder,
And makes a noise like father's gun,
  Only a nation louder.

I went as nigh to one myself
  As 'Siah's underpinning ;
And father went as nigh agin,
  I thought the deuce was in him.

Cousin Simon grew so bold
  I thought he would have cock'd it ;
It scar'd me so, I shrink'd it off
  And hung by father's pocket.

And Captain Davis had a gun,
  He kind of clapt his hand on't,
And stuck a crooked stabbing iron
  Upon the little end on't.

And there I see a pumpkin-shell
  As big as mother's bason;
And every time they touched it off
  They scampered like the nation.

I see a little barrel, too,
  The heads were made of leather,
They knock'd upon't with little clubs
  And call'd the folks together.

And there was Captain Washington
  Upon a slapping stallion,
A-giving orders to his men—
  I guess there was a million.

And then the feathers on his hat,
  They looked so tarnal fina,
I wanted pockily to get
  To give to my Jemima.

And there they'd fife away like fun,
  And play on cornstalk fiddles,
And some had ribbons red as blood
  All wound about their middles.

The troopers, too, would gallop up,
  And fire right in our faces;
It scar'd me almost half to death
  To see them run such races.

Old Uncle Sam come there to change
  Some pancakes and some onions
For 'lasses-cake, to carry home
  To give his wife and young ones.
  10

But I can't tell you half I see,
They kept up such a smother;
So I took my hat off, made a bow,
And scampered home to mother.

VI.

THE STATE HOUSE.

From Miss Polly Ingham to Dr. Hale.

DEAR DR. HALE : Please remember that Mamma is occupied some days with her lunch parties and committee meetings and things, so that perhaps she can not go with us young people at all. Can you not give us a list of little sights that we could go to separately without dragging poor mamma out with us? Always truly yours,   POLLY INGHAM.

[Little Polly.]

MY DEAR POLLY : You are very practical and wise, as I observe you always are. This list shall be of visits near at hand, which you can make with your sisters or your brother, or Miss Lovechild, without any chaperon.

105

Recollect what I told you about the street cars. I told you then how the first thing Dr. Stanley did was to go to the cupola of the State House. And the last thing he did was to go there again and review all he had learned.

I advise you to go to the State House first. If you hit the right day they will let you go up to the cupola. If there is any difficulty you can ask for the sergeant-at-arms, who is very nice and pleasant, and say that you have come all the way from New Padua and perhaps you can never come again. I think he will let you go up.

But I do not think you will have to ask for him. And for young people like you, who have climbed the monument yonder, and are one day going to the top of the cathedral at Milan, this is no hardship.

At the top—well, you can see "as far as the eye will reach !" That is true in most places, but here it means—oh ! more than fifty miles in many directions. Take this panorama, with what you have seen from

Bunker Hill, and you have a very good idea of the "lay of the land" and the water.

Seaward you see what is called Massachusetts Bay in your geographies. In the first generation they gave the name of Massachusetts Bay to the head of the bay, which lies right before you—what we now call Boston Harbor.

And we distinguish between the outer harbor and the inner harbor. Governor Winthrop called this inner harbor, which is close to you, The Loch, but no one has called it so since, except me. But it is, as you see, land-*locked*. Deer Island—there where you see the great buildings—and Long Island— there where you see a lighthouse—separate it from the outer harbor. Yonder, far away, is the white outer lighthouse, and beyond that Massachusetts Bay—as we have the phrase to-day—and the ocean.

Unfold that nice map, and fix it right by Paul's compass, and you can find Charlestown, and Cambridge, and Brighton, and Brookline, and Dorchester, and the towns beyond. If you want to remember the order of the names, Polly, recollect that Boston, where you are, begins with B. Then go west, and there is Brighton. Go south, and you come to Brookline and Dorchester, in alphabetical order observe. Go north and east, and you come to Cambridge, Charlestown, and Chelsea, still in alphabetical order. All of these, except Cambridge, Chelsea, and Brookline, are under the same government as Boston. Cambridge and Chelsea are separate cities, each with its own charter, mayor, and councils. Brookline has what we call a town government.

Perhaps you will spend all the afternoon here. But if it is foggy there is quite enough to occupy you in the other parts of the State House. The attendants there are all courteous, and they will show you what you ask for. Be sure you see the new Representatives' Chamber, and, in the older part, the old Senate Chamber and the new Senate Chamber, and the Governor's Room.

Ask for the Library and the Archive

Chamber. As soon as they see that you are intelligent girls and know what you want, they will be very glad to answer any of your questions. Try to think, before you go, what you want to ask—perhaps about your great-grandfather's service when he was in the privateer Yankee Lass, or ask them to show you General Gates's letter in which he announces Burgoyne's surrender. Or they will show you some of Franklin's autographs when he was our commissioner in London.

I remember tracing along from page to page, on the great books in which the original letters are preserved, the petition of a nice person, evidently a prudent housekeeper, that she might have back again the overcoat which her husband wore on the day of the battle of Bunker Hill. Poor soul, she seemed never to have seen her husband again, and she had never seen his overcoat; and she had a feeling that the General Court ought to send the overcoat back to her. But the matter fades out of history, and I am afraid she never saw it, and never received the money that it cost.

Here is a vote of the 15th of June, two days before the battle, foreshadowing the seizure of Dorchester Heights, which was carried out so well the next spring by Washington and Ward and Thomas. Why the English commanders did not take possession of an eminence so absolutely necessary, if their navy was to remain in the harbor, nobody knows. They had a very large army in Boston; this army was very badly cooped up there, and Dorchester Heights would have been an admirable camp for the whole summer and autumn. But, for some reason, they neglected to seize it, and left it for Washington to take in March, when the building of the works there was the signal for General William Howe's retirement from Boston:

"Whereas it appears of importance to the Safety of this Colony that possession of the Hill called Bunker's Hill in Charlestown be securely kept and defended and also Some one Hill or Hills on Dorchester Neck be likewise Secured, therefore Resolved unanimously that it be recommended to the Council of

War, that the above mentioned Bunker Hill
be maintained by sufficient force being posted
there, and as the particular Situation of Dorchester Neck is unknown to this Committee,
they advise that the Council of War take and
pursue such steps respecting the same as to
them shall appear to be for the Security of
this Colony."

Here is the draft of an early circular letter
to the different colonies:

"On the same day the town of Charlestown consisting of near five hundred houses
and other buildings was by those bloody in-
cendiaries set on fire and consumed to ashes,
we cannot however but assure you, gentlemen
that notwithstanding our present distressed
situation, we feel a peculiar satisfaction in
finding our patriotic brethren of the city and
county of Albany so cordially interesting
themselves in our particular welfare and so
kindly offering us their assistance as well as
manifesting their zeal for the rights and liberties of America in general. It is our ardent
desire to cultivate harmony and friendship

with all our neighboring brethren and we
hope you will not fail to continue your fa-
vors and we assure you that we shall always
take pleasure in conveying to you any intelli-
gence that shall afford satisfaction. As to
the benevolent donations you mention which
are collected for our distressed brethren, as
the transporting the article you make mention of is almost impossible, think it had better be exchanged for cash or some necessary
specie which may be more easily transported.
We are sorry to hear there is any prospects
of an attack upon Tyconderoga, &c., but we
trust those important fortresses are sufficient-
ly garrisoned and doubt not but our brave
countrymen stationed there will be able to
repulse any force which can be sent against
them from Canada. Finally, brethren we ar-
dently pray that the Great Supreme being
who Governs all things may so Direct all our
military operations that they may Speedily
Issue in the full Restoration and Peaceable
Possession of the Natural and Constitutional
Rights and Liberties of every American."

acts by them done (this their condition considered) might be as firme as any patent; and in some respects more sure. The forme was as followeth.

In ye name of God Amen· We whose names are vnderwriten, the loyall subiects of our dread soueraigne Lord King Iames, by ye grace of God, of great Britaine, franc, & Ireland king, defendor of ye faith, &c

Haueing vndertaken, for ye glorie of God, and aduancemente of ye christian faith, and honour of our king & countrie, a voyage to plant ye first colonie in ye Northerne parts of Virginia· doe by these presents solemnly & mutualy in ye presence of God, and one of another; couenant, & combine our selues togeather into a ciuill body politick; for ye our better ordering, & preseruation & furtherance of ye ends aforesaid; and by vertue hearof to enacte, constitute, and frame shuch just & equall Lawes, ordinances, Acts, constitutions, & offices, from time to time, as shall be thought most meete & conuenient for ye generall good of ye Colonie. vnto which we promise all due submission and obedience· In witnes wherof we haue here vnder subscribed our names at Cap-Codd ye ·11· of Nouember, in ye year of ye raigne of our soueraigne Lord king Iames of England, franc, & Ireland ye eighteenth and of Scotland ye fiftie fourth· An: Dom ·1620·]

After this they chose, or rather confirmed mr John Carner (a man godly & well approued amongst them) their Gouernour for that year· And after they had prouided a place for their goods, or comons Store, (which were long in vnlading for want of boats, foulnes of ye winter weather, and sicknes of diuers) and begune some small cottages for their habitation; as time would admitte, they mette and consulted of Lawes, & orders, both for their ciuill & military gouermente, as ye necesitie of their condition did require, still adding thervnto as vrgent occasion in severall times, and as cases did require.

In these hard & difficulte beginings they found some discontents & murmurings amongst some, and mutinous speeches & cariags in other; but they were soone quelled, & ouercome, by ye wisdome, patience, and just & equall carrage of things, by ye gour. nd better part wch clave faithfuly togeather in ye maine. But that which was most sadd, & lamentable, was, that in 2 & 3 monoths time halfe of their company dyed, espeatly in Ian: & february, being ye deptle of winter, and wanting houses & other comforts; being infected with ye scuruie &

Stop, as you go down, in the Secretary of State's office and ask if you may see the charters. They will show you the first charter which Winthrop brought over, and the province charter which was granted by William III. Perhaps you can see the original Bradford manuscript, which we have just now recovered from London. It is the history of the first settlement of Plymouth, as dear old William Bradford—your ancestor, Polly, on your mother's side, through the Woodbridge line:—dear old William Bradford, I say, wrote it out in Plymouth or Duxbury.

All depends on weather. Very likely you will have spent all the afternoon in the State House. If so, we will put off the other home walks to another day.

When, in 1746, the immense armada of D'Anville crossed the water to destroy Boston, Governor Shirley and the Boston people were taken wholly by surprise. A little fisherman ran in of a sudden to say that

he had seen such a squadron as he never
saw before. Well he might, for it was, I
think, the largest fleet which ever sailed
from Europe to America up to this day.
What is interesting now is that, of the
preparations for war for the next six weeks,
you will read nothing in the Boston news-
papers of that day, excepting the pathetic
words which say that the train bands of
the province followed to the grave the body
of the young and beautiful wife of Governor
Shirley.

How happened it that the train bands of
the province were there? Why, it was because Shirley had ordered them to Boston to
meet the French, and they were encamped
on Boston Common—the largest body of
troops who were ever on Boston Common at
one time.

For the rest, no newspaper mentions the
blocking up of the harbor, no newspaper
mentions the arrival of these train bands.
You would not know that for those weeks
Boston was in terror. But if you have time

to ask for the Council Records of 1746, you will find here the whole story.

When the people of Boston were engaged, a few years ago, in preserving the Old South Meeting House as a memorial of this crisis, I sent to Mr. Henry W. Longfellow the account given of it by Thomas Prince, the minister of the Old South. Mr. Longfellow was delighted with Prince's account of the Fast Day for which Shirley issued his proclamation on the occasion, and wrote for the Old South Association his Ballad of the French Fleet, which in my judgment is the best of his ballads. And this Polly may read aloud to her mother this evening :

A BALLAD OF THE FRENCH FLEET.

October, 1746.

Mr. Thomas Prince, *loquitur.*

A fleet with flags arrayed
    Sailed from the port of Brest,
And the Admiral's ship displayed
    The signal : "Steer southwest."
For this Admiral d'Anville
    Had sworn by cross and crown
To ravage with fire and steel
    Our helpless Boston Town.

There were rumors in the street,
In the houses there was fear
Of the coming of the fleet,
And the danger hovering near.
And while from mouth to mouth
Spread the tidings of dismay,
I stood in the Old South,
Saying humbly, " Let us pray.

" O Lord ! we would not advise ;
But if, in thy providence,
A tempest should arise
To drive the French fleet hence,
And scatter it far and wide,
Or sink it in the sea,
We should be satisfied,
And thine the glory be."

This was the prayer I made,
For my soul was all on flame ;
And even as I prayed
The answering tempest came.
It came with a mighty power,
Shaking the windows and walls,
And tolling the bell in the tower
As it tolls at funerals.

The lightning suddenly
Unsheathed its flaming sword,
And I cried, " Stand still and see
The salvation of the Lord ! "
The heavens were black with cloud,
The sea was white with hail,
And ever more fierce and loud
Blew the October gale.

The fleet it overtook,
  And the broad sails in the van
Like the tents of Cushan shook,
  Or the curtains of Midian.
Down on the reeling decks
  Crashed the o'erwhelming seas;
Ah, never were there wrecks
  So pitiful as these!

Like a potter's vessel broke
  The great ships of the line;
They were carried away as a smoke,
  Or sank like lead in the brine.
O Lord! before thy path
  They vanished and ceased to be,
When thou didst walk in wrath
  With thine horses through the sea!

VII

ANOTHER DAY IN OLD BOSTON.

IF there is time to read an old-fashioned
novel evenings or on rainy days, you might
ask at the hotel library for Lionel Lincoln,
by one Cooper, of whom you have heard, perhaps. Cooper saw what you see—oh, as far
back as the first twenty years of this century.
And the book will give you some idea of the
Boston of that day, as of the Revolutionary
days.

Suppose we start from the State House
on another walk. Leave the Common this
time and go northward through Beacon Street.
Here is the Boston Athenæum, and though
we have no time to go into the library, we
will just look into the entrance hall, where
is a cast of Houdon's Washington and some
good portraits.

Now walk on, turn a little to the right, and go down hill. You pass the new and old Congregational Houses. Now just here, Paul, is where the schoolboys started on their coast, as dear Mr. Robins told me the story. "Lickety cut—clear the lalla—clear the coast!"—I dare say they shouted just as they do now. That victory of theirs, with General Haldimand, was the first victory of the Revolution. I tried to make the mayor proclaim a holiday for the last week in every January—a holiday in which every Boston boy might coast down this street as far as Washington Street.

Cross Tremont Street. On the right, where Parker's Hotel is, was the schoolhouse of those days. But it was on the left-hand side—on the north side—when Benjamin Franklin went to school there—the Franklin of the whistle. Do not pass his statue, which stands where he used to play "tag," without looking at it carefully. The Franklin is, on the whole, the best bronze statue in Boston, though, if you want to, you may

speak of Powers's Webster in the same day.
Remember what I told you, that Mr. Greenough modeled the head in conformity with
his own acute observation, that one side of
Franklin's face showed him as the good-
natured, shrewd humorist, as "Poor Richard,"
while the other side shows the grave philoso-
pher and statesman. Observe the fur: fur,
Mr. Greenough tells me, was a printer's
badge. The other statue is by Ball. It rep-
resents the first Mayor Quincy, the same who
was president of Harvard College. He was
the son of Josiah Quincy, of the Revolution,
and was the great-grandfather of Josiah
Quincy, who is the Mayor in 1898, when
these words are written.

Court Street was Queen Street in more
loyal times, named, I think, from Queen
Anne—perhaps from Queen Caroline, of the
Heart of Midlothian. When it crosses Washington Street it becomes State Street. In
the loyal days it became King Street. But
in 1776 we changed all that. In that same
1776, for reasons well known to you, we

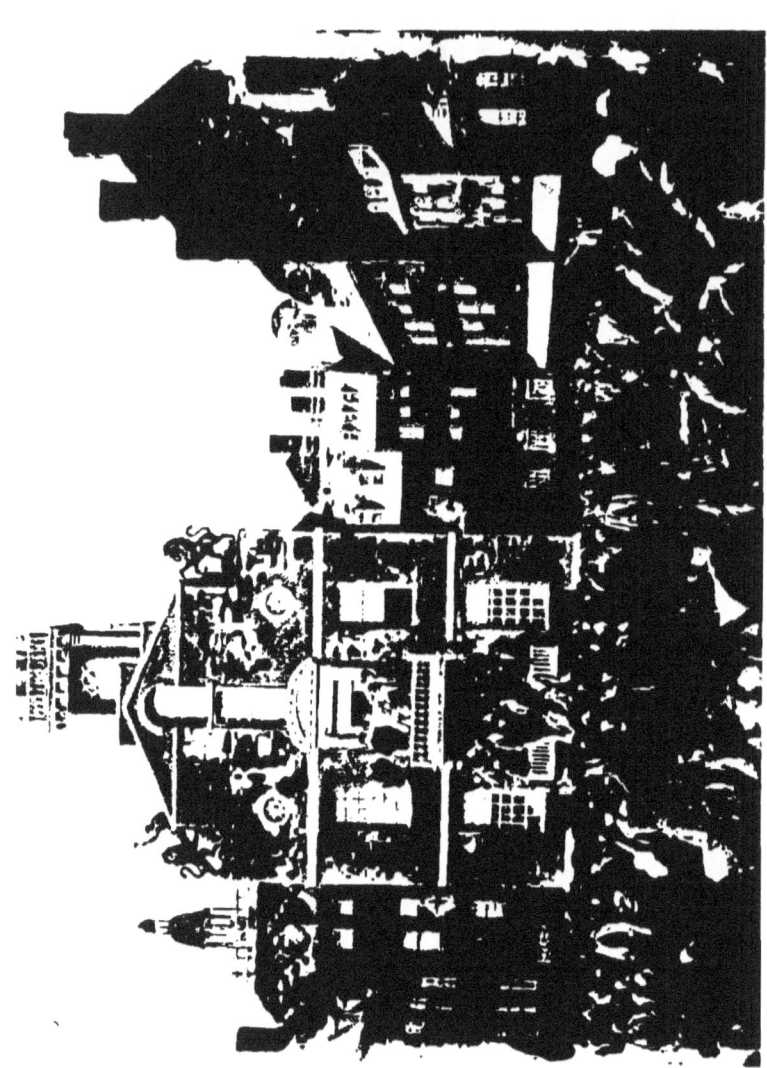

Reading the Declaration of Independence.

(Old State House.)

took down the lion and the unicorn from
the State House, although you now see them
there again, "fighting for the crown," as in
the nursery song. We put them up a few
years ago as matter of history, and a stanch
Irish member of the council insisted, wittily
and wisely, I think, that history should also
be represented by our putting up the American eagle over their heads. So you may see
a "happy family" of the three.

Let us cross over by this foot walk to
Court Square and Court Street.

Walk down State Street still, by the old
building, but do not leave the narrow side-
walk. You see the scene of the Boston
massacre. At your left, at the corner of Ex-
change Street, stood the file of English soldiers—"lobster backs," as the mob called
them—whom the mob insulted. On your
right, on the north side of the street, the mob
hooted them and pelted them. The soldiers
fired, at Preston's order, and nine men were
killed. Above you, on the second story, is
the balcony from which Colonel Crafts or

Mr. Greenleaf read the Declaration of Independence.

Now go back a few steps and go upstairs into the dear old State House itself, and see the rooms where the Council and Assembly sat in the old days. After the constitution of the State was formed, the House of Representatives and Senate sat here. Here you will have your fill of interesting curiosities collected by the Bostonian Society. It was in the Council Chamber that James Otis made his famous speech on the "Writs of Assistance," of which John Adams says that "then and there American independence was born."

Walk down State Street to Broad Street, and take your right. Any policeman will tell you how to walk along, on what is now Commercial Street, till you come to the bronze tablet, well designed, which tells where the tea was thrown overboard. Do not ask for T Wharf; that is another sort of T.

Now you have seen the best two of the Revolutionary buildings; for I count the two

State Houses as such, though the new State House was not begun till the new nation had become prosperous and had gone about its business. I call it so because Sam Adams laid the corner stone, because it contains the old relics from Bennington and other battle-fields, and because the unprinted history of the war is there.

Another Revolutionary building is the Old South Meeting-House, which is the " nursery of freedom," and another is Christ Church, in Salem Street, the lantern church, of which I have spoken.

The Italians now make the ruling popu-lation in the neighborhood of the lantern church. They do not know much of history, but they are equal to the emergency, and they have created a myth of their own. They see a crowd of people assemble on the 19th of April to look at the church and to hear the chime as it plays the national air. And the story-tellers among them will tell you that in the old days, long, long ago, the people of Boston became very wicked, and

forgot God and heaven and hell and the angels and all saints. And so, one night, the
Virgin Mary descended from heaven and
hung a lantern on the steeple, that all men
and women might see and believe. From
that time to this, according to the legend, the
people of Boston have been the comparatively
decent people that they are now, with a certain reverence for sacred things.

These things, therefore, the Italians will
tell you. If you care to extend your walk
from Christ Church, you will find the new
park where these little Italian children can
paddle in the dear old sea. If you have my
luck on my last walk there, you will hear
some North End children sing, "Onery, Two-
ery," with a loyal refrain about the king and
queen which some sailor ancestor learned
nearly two hundred years ago. The king
and queen were William and Mary.

Later than sixty years ago, as you have
seen, the outer works of the English were
visible, where Blackstone and Franklin
Squares are now. The committee on public

Christ Church.

grounds might well renew them before another winter comes, and put one of the old
captured cannon on each of them.

And in Roxbury, on Fort Hill Avenue, is
a good reproduction of Knox's "upper fort,"
of which the most exaggerated accounts were
printed in Europe. In South Boston is Independence Square, where you may get an
idea of the fortifications which compelled the
English to evacuate the town. *Hostibus primo
fugatis* is the motto on the medal which Congress then gave to Washington. This medal
is now in the cabinet of the Historical Society.
But you had better reserve the visit to Independence Square to another day.

A good experience would be to come into
town on Washington Street, as the army
came in triumph on the morning of March 17,
1776. We should thus reverse our ride of
the day we went to Lexington. The British
squadron had left, with the refugee Tories
and their families. Washington, with a large
force, marched in over the Neck. And from
that time that part of the street was named

Washington Street. The name has since absorbed all the old names of different parts of the same highway—Orange Street, Newbury Street, Marlboro Street—which recall so many different passages of history.

Take any outward-bound car on Washington Street, and ask to be dropped at the old car stable. It is just at the point where, as an old stone shows you, Boston once ended and Roxbury began. Here it was that, when Washington was President, he waited in a cold northeaster while the Selectmen and Governor Hancock settled some quarrel of etiquette. "Is there no other way into the town?" said the President at last, and the uneasy procession moved. But then and there the people caught the "Washington influenza," which has its place in history.

Take any open car that is bound northward. At Blackstone and Franklin Squares you will pass the point where were the advanced English works, spoken of on page 124. At Dover Street was a gate, with a picket fence. Beach Street, when you come

to it, preserves the memory of the beach,
which is well remembered by that old gentleman in front of you; very likely he has
"gone in swimming" there.   Look up at the
right just as you come to Sage's trunk store
at the corner of Boylston Street, and you see,
in stone, the representation of the Liberty
Tree of the Revolution.

Farther on, you might get off at Milk
Street, walk a few steps back, then turn into
a queer dark alley, and see all that is left of
the Province House, which you know so well
from Hawthorne.   The Old South itself, in
Milk Street, is one of the few historical buildings spared.   Opposite, in Milk Street, a tablet will tell you where Franklin was born.
The legend is that he was put in a silk bag
before he was twelve hours old, and carried
across the street for Mr. Willard to christen
him.

When Burgoyne was riding into Boston,
after his surrender, General Heath, the American commander here, accompanied him.
"There is the Governor's house," said Bur-

goyne, as they passed it. "Yes," said a rude boy who jostled them, "and on the other side is the riding school." For when Burgoyne was in Boston before, the cavalry had used the Old South for a school of horsemanship.

I believe you have been in the old meeting-house. The steeple is the same which shook in the October gale of Mr. Longfellow's ballad, when—

> It tolled the bell in the tower
> As it tolls for funerals.

Walk on; let the cars go down Milk Street. At the corner of School Street you see the Old Corner Bookstore, very little changed since Longfellow and the Mutual Admiration Society met there, and Fields and Whipple and Warren Sawyer and that young set met Holmes and Lowell and Parsons and Hawthorne there. Go a little farther, and you come to the old State House again.

On the upper corner, on one side, was General Knox's bookshop. Opposite was the

12

The Province House.

best inn in town in 1776. I think Howe
had his quarters there; I know that Washington took up his there, after his army en-
tered.

He took the landlady's little daughter on
his knee. "Well, little lady, you have seen
the English soldiers, and now you see the
Yankees—which do you like best?"

Children are not good liars, and on Washington's knee no one, I suppose, could tell a
lie. The child said truly that she liked the
redcoats best.

The general laughed. "Yes, indeed," he
said, "they have the best clothes. But it
takes the ragged boys to do the fighting."
This story the little girl's daughter told me
in 1857.

And here, dear Polly, we must stop. But
perhaps you can find your way alone to
Copp's Hill, and poke about among the tombs
and graves there. Here Gage and Burgoyne
watched the fight at Bunker Hill, where
Howe, then Gage's subordinate, was leading
the right wing up to the rail fence. And

here the well-informed janitor will tell you his stories.

One must stop somewhere. I have given you what you may take in six or seven days. Some of the churches will be open on week days. Among those of historical interest are the First Church, where you will see the original broad covenant of the church emblazoned on one of the windows; the Second Church, where the Mathers preached, where Emerson and Henry Ware have preached since then; the Third Church, on the corner of Copley Square, which used to meet in the Old South Meeting-House which you have visited. King's Chapel was the first Episcopal church; Arlington Street Church was the first Presbyterian church.

The First Baptist Church, though not in its old place, worships in the fine church at the corner of Clarendon Street and Commonwealth Avenue. Bartholdi, the famous sculptor, executed the designs of the statues on the tower of that church; he told me himself that the heads which you will see there are

portraits of distinguished citizens of Boston of
that time. If you buy the right photographs,
and magnify them with the right glasses,
you will find Sumner and, I think, Garrison,
and probably Everett and Phillips. The first
Catholic church was in Milk Street; the Cathedral is now nearly opposite Union Park, on
Washington Street, where water flowed in the
days when the good Cheverus really established the first Roman Catholic church.

When you visit Rome, if you see the Holy
Father, he will ask you how long you are
going to stay in Rome. If you say "seven
days," he will say, "You can see a great deal
of Rome in seven days." If you say "six
months," he will say, "You will be beginning
to be acquainted in six months." If you say
"two years," he will say, "Ah, when you
leave us you will say you know nothing about
us!" I might say very much the same of
Boston. And as I want to encourage you, I
will intimate that in seven days you may see
a good deal of the dear old town.

If Pauline needs anything to read to-night

she may read the ballad of the Old South,
which, in a way, sums up this history:

THE OLD SOUTH MEETING-HOUSE.

To hide the time-stains on our wall,
Let every tattered banner fall!
The Bourbon lilies, green and old,
That flaunted once, in burnished gold;
The oriflamme of France that fell
That day when sun-burned Pepperell
His shotted salvos fired so well.
The Fleur de Lys trailed sulky down,
And Louisburg was George's town.
The Bourbon yields it, in despair,
To Saxon arm and Pilgrim prayer.

Hang there the Lion and the Tower,
The trophies of an earlier hour,
Pale emblems of Castilian pride,
That shrouded Winslow when he died
    Beneath Jamaica's palm.

Hang there, and there, the dusty rags
Which once were jaunty battle-flags,
And, for a week, in triumph vain,
Gay flaunted over blue Champlain;
Gayly had circled half the world,
Until they drooped, disgraced and furled
    That day the Hampshire line
Stood to its arms at dress parade,
Beneath the Stars and Stripes arrayed,
    And Massachusetts Pine,
To see the great atonement made
By " Ried'sel " and Burgoyne.

King's Chapel.

Eagles which Cæsar's hand had fed,
Banners which Charlemagne had led
  A thousand years before,
A dozing empire meanly gave
To grace a court or serve a slave ;
Let Brunswick and the Landgrave wave
  Their banners on our shore.
Brunswick and Hesse basely sold
Eagle and flag for George's gold ;
  And in the storm of war,
In crash of battle, thick and dark,
Beneath the rifle-shot of Stark,
The war-worn staves, the crests of gold,
The 'scutcheons proud, the storied fold,
In surges of defeat were rolled !—
So, even Roman banners fall
To screen the time-stains on our wall !

Beneath the war-flags' faded fold
I see our sovereigns of old
  On magic canvas there.
The tired face of "baby Charles"
Looks sadly down from Pilgrim walls,
  Half pride and half despair,
Doubtful to flatter or to strike,
  To cozen or to dare.
His steel-clad charger he bestrides,
As if to smite the Ironsides,
When Rupert with his squadron rides;
Yet, such his gloomy brow and eye,
You wonder if he will not try
Once more the magic of a lie
  To lift him from his care.

Hold still your truncheon! If it moves,
  The ire of Cromwell's rage it braves!
For the next picture shows
The grim Protector on his steed,
Ready to pray, to strike, to lead,—
  Dare all for England, which he saves,
New England, which he loves.

These are Vandyck's. 'Tis Kneller there
Has pictured a more peaceful pair:
There Orange gives his last command,
The Charter gives to Mather's hand;
And, blooming there, the queenly she
Who takes, "now counsel, and now tea,"
Confounding Blenheim and Bohea,
  Careless of war's alarm.
Yet, as of old, the virgin Queen,
When armed for victory, might press
The smoky firelock of " Brown Bess,"
So Anna, in a fond caress,
  Rests on a black " Queen's arm."

Beneath those forms another band,
Silent, but eloquent, shall stand.
There is no uttered voice nor speech
As still of liberty they teach;
No language and no sound is heard,
Yet still the everlasting word
Goes forth to thrill the land.

Story and Greenough shall compel
The silent marble form to tell
The lesson that they told so well—
  Lessons of Fate and Awe;

Franklin still point the commonplace
  Of Liberty and Law.
Adams shall look in Otis' face
  Blazing with Freedom's soul,
And Molyneux see Hancock trace
The fatal word which frees a race,
There, in New England's well-earned place,
  The head of Freedom's roll.

VIII

THE ISLANDS AND THE FORTS.

PERHAPS mamma will be afraid of being upset in a boat and drowned. Perhaps she will be afraid that the boys and girls will be.

But if not—if mamma and papa are both disposed to take a comfortable boat, with a skillful skipper, at one of the boat landings— I will tell you of a very pleasant excursion which you may make, all of you, and you shall come home safe, and you shall thank me for giving you the hint.

I should say that as good a way to begin as any, would be to take one of the street cars which goes out to the eastern end of South Boston. If you find you are in another South Boston car, transfer into something which will take you to the Marine Park at City Point. There let papa look

Squantum Head.

round and find a good skipper and a good boat, and hire them for the afternoon. You had better start pretty early. But do not let any boy go and do this unless papa is present. I do not respect the judgment of Fred Junior as much as I do that of his father.

When you are all on board the boat, tell the skipper that you want to go down to Squantum and see the bold point there where, "they do say," an Indian squaw threw herself into the sea. For my part, I do not believe that there could have been so many Sapphos who threw themselves into the sea because the rocks were high, as popular tradition supposes. But here is a bold fine bluff of stone; and here is a monument, because this is the point where Captain Standish, and perhaps Edward Winslow, landed in September, 1621. And here they found some lobsters, and they boiled the lobsters and ate them. And afterward they found the women who owned the lobster pots, and they paid the women for the lobsters and they went their way.

Now this was the first expedition of
white men, or of any other men, who have
left any record that they even so much as
saw our dear Boston. The famous Champlain, the Frenchman, came down here more
than ten years before ; but he did not put
down Boston on his map with any such precision that it can be recognized. Captain
John Smith—the same who was saved by
Pocahontas and who cut off the heads of
three Turks—came up the bay a little after
Champlain. He said there were many islands here, as there are ; and he put down
Charles River, but he does not seem to have
landed in Boston. But in this September,
1621, which I told you about, the Pilgrim
Fathers at Plymouth, wishing that they
knew more of what they called the head of
the bay, sent up this shallop, as they called
it, with some people on board, of whom the
military commander was Miles Standish.
And, although there is the least bit of a
quarrel about it, I think the other commander was Edward Winslow—yes, Mary,

he is the same who died afterward on his way to Jamaica. The Spanish colors

> Shrouded Winslow when he died,—
> Beneath Jamaica's palm.

After they had had that feast of lobsters, they sailed north and must have passed by the whole front of Boston. But they do not seem to have landed there; they do not say that they landed there. On the other hand, we know that they did pass the whole eastern front of Charlestown; they must have looked up and seen Bunker's Hill, but they did not know it was to be called Bunker's Hill, and they did not know there was to be a battle there. They went on and on, and at a point which perhaps the boatman will know about, about two miles north of the navy yard or somewhere in that region, they landed. And this is the first landing of white people which anybody knows anything about, on what is now the territorial domain of Boston. And perhaps this is not on the territorial domain of Boston; perhaps this is a little

13

farther up, and is in the town of Somerville. Anyway, they found here on poles the dead body of Nanepashemet, a sachem who had died not long before. And here also they found some courageous Indian women, with whom they had courteous interchange of such things as the women had to sell, and as they wanted to buy.

Alas, they have left very little account of what they saw! But here is an account which Bradford, who sent them out, wrote about an early expedition of his. I think we may say that there is no earlier description of Boston than is in the third, fourth, and fifth lines of this poem :

O Boston, though thou now art grown
To be a great and wealthy town,
Yet I have seen thee a void place,
Shrubs and bushes covering thy face ;
And house then in thee none were there,
Nor such as gold and silk did weare ;
No drunkenness were then in thee,
Nor such excesse as now we see.
We then drunk freely of thy spring
Without paying of anything ;
We lodged freely where we would,
All things were free and nothing sold.

And they that did thee first begin
Had hearts as free and as willing
Their poor friends for to entertaine,
And never looked at sordid gaine.
Some thou hast had whome I did know,
That spent theirselves to make thee grow,
And thy foundations they did lay
Which doe remaine unto this day.
When thou wast weak they did thee nurse,
Or else with thee it had been worse ;
They left not thee, but did defend
And succour thee until their end.
Thou now hast growne in wealth and store,
Do not forget that thou wast poore,
And lift not up thyself in pride,
From truth and justice turn not aside.
Remember thou a Cotton had,
Which made the hearts of many glad ;
What he thee taught bear thou in minde,
It's hard another such to finde.
A Winthrop once in thee was knowne,
Who unto thee was as a crowne.
Such ornaments are very rare,
Yet thou enjoyed this blessed pair.
But these are gone, their work is done,
Their day is past, set is their sun :
Yet faithful Wilson still remains,
And learned Norton doth take pains.
Live ye in peace. I could say more.
Oppress ye not the weake and poore.
The trade is all in your own hand,
Take heede ye doe not wrong the land,
Lest he that hath lift you on high,
Whenas the poore to him doe cry,

Doe throw you downe from your high state,
And make you low and desolate.

Now, as you come home, if this boatman
whom I have recommended says there is
time, ask him to take you down, first to Gov-
ernör's Island and then to Castle Island, and
you shall see the two fortified places which
for about two hundred years protected, or
tried to protect, our town of Boston from
foreign invasion.

You will see that Governor's Island is
not a large island, and if they will let you
land, you will be able to go in to see the
curious fortification which is now established
there. You can hardly see it from the sea;
you might even think it was the roof of an
old barn. But in fact there is a strong fort
there, and the reason you do not see more is
that it is, so to speak, sunk in the ground
and protected from the shots of an enemy by
the very hill which once made a part of the
island. Such are the habits of modern en-
gineers.

This little island was originally called

Fort Winthrop. Governor's Island.

Conant's Island. I suppose it was named from Richard Conant, who is one of the four men who are generally spoken of as the first four settlers of Massachusetts Bay. But I do not know, and perhaps nobody else knows. Very early it was given to our good John Winthrop, who was the first Governor of Massachusetts after the arrival of the settlers of 1630. He is the Governor Winthrop who brought the charter over with him, whom you will see represented at the head of Court Street with the charter in his hand. And, if you make this trip after the expedition to the State House, as perhaps you will, you will like to remember that the charter which he brought is the oldest of the charters which you have seen there.

The General Court gave him the island, and they called it "Governor's Island." He did not think of a fort there then; they all thought it was going to be a sort of vine-yard. They did not know then how poor the grapes were which grew here. So they

gave it, I think as a sort of a joke, to him
for forty shillings ; but he was to pay one
shilling rent on the 25th of March. It was
also agreed that he should plant a vineyard
and an orchard there. And it was agreed
that after his death the lease should be renewed for twenty-one years to his heirs ; only
that the heirs should pay a fifth part of the
fruits which should be yearly raised out of
the same. I think this is their only grant of
land on such queer, old-fashioned conditions.
And the reason why I think so is that, after
a year or two, the lease was changed. I
think they had all been down the bay together, Winthrop and the rest ; for they then
passed a vote that, " Whereas, the yearly rent
was the fifth part of all the fruits that shall
grow there, it is ordered, at the request of
John Winthrop, Esquire, that the rent of
said island shall be a hogshead of the best
wine that shall grow there, to be paid yearly
after his death, and nothing before." Then
afterward (I rather think they had been
down the harbor again to see it, and had

found that the wine was not likely to be very good) they confirmed the grant on condition that the rent should be only two bushels of apples every year—one bushel to the Governor and another to the General Court, "the same to be of the best apples there growing."

All this seems a little as if it were fun; and accordingly we find, on another occasion, that the Governor paid a bushel of apples to the General Court, although it would seem by the terms of the grant that they were only to be paid after his death. On some such terms as these the island was granted to him, and it remained in the possession of some representatives of his family until the United States bought it, within the present century, and established upon it a fort, which is called Fort Winthrop to this day.

Land there, as I say, if you have time and if they will let you; but if there is not time enough for both, go across to the landing at Fort Independence. The fort which now has this name is established where the Castle William of the last century was built, and this castle was named after William III. Up till that time the fortification here was generally called "the Castle" and had no other name.

When the first settlers came to Boston they took their chances against a foreign enemy; but they had not been there many years when La Tour, a Frenchman, came to Boston to solicit aid against his countrymen in Acadia. The arrival of his ship gave a great alarm to the town, for so little attention had been paid to defense that there was not a soldier on the island. In consequence of this surprise the fort was rebuilt at the expense of the six neighboring towns and garrisoned principally from Dorchester. It still showed the weakness or the economy of the colony. It was made of wood, and in 1665 had not more than six guns mounted.

It had been proposed at first to have a "floating galley," as they called it, forty feet long and twenty feet wide, and some of the

liberal people subscribed for that. But before the summer was over they changed their
minds about this and the fort was built instead; and this was the first of a series of
seven fortifications which were built at different crises here, of which the last is Fort
Independence, which you shall now see.
We peace people like to say that the forts
have done their duty without ever firing a
shot in anger. Once or twice there has been
a shot fired across the bows of some vessel
that was coming in, to make her show her
colors or account for herself in some way;
but no enemy but Time has ever attacked
either of the different forts. And, last of
all, we went to Congress and asked Congress to give us back our whole island for
a playground for our children, and then Congress did so.

The island is called Castle Island, and always has been called Castle Island. When
the nation was established the State of Massachusetts gave the island to the General Government, and now the General Government

has given back the use of the island to the city of Boston for a part of its public-park system.

Perhaps all this about the boat and the skipper and the sailing across the harbor may prove imaginary. Perhaps the day is not nice, or perhaps mamma has to attend a meeting of the Colonial Dames, so that only the boys and girls can go. In that case you can still see the fort and can walk about and can look across and see Winthrop's island; and, I think, if you get on the highest point of all, you can see far off the point at Squantum where the lobsters were.

You will take some South Boston car, as I have described before; but, instead of asking for a boat at City Point, ask one of the guides to show you the pretty pier which goes across the water to the island. It will please you to see the number of little children running about on the pier, and to see the little white babies sitting on their mothers' knees and taking the comfort of the sea air.

Fort Independence.

In 1665, as dear old Captain Richard Davenport, who was the commander of the Castle, was taking his afternoon nap on the 15th of July, he was struck dead by lightning. His dog was killed at the gate. There was only a wainscot partition between his room and the magazine of powder. He was an old man who had had to do with that incident which I think you have read about, when, thirty years before, Endicott had cut the cross out of the king's colors. From that time to his time it had been agreed that the red cross should be shown in the flag at the Castle, while it was not shown anywhere on the mainland until the reign of Charles II. Captain Richard Clap, who has given one of the most quaint accounts of the early settlement left from that generation, was appointed as Davenport's successor. In 1673 the whole fort was burned down by accident and a stone fort was then built in its place. After King William came to the throne he sent over Colonel Romer, a celebrated engineer, to repair the fort. Instead of repairing it, he demolished

the old works and raised an entirely new fortification.

Of this new fort, Dummer, in his Defense
of New England Charters, page 17, gives a minute description. He says: "At the entrance
of the harbor there is a strong, beautiful Castle which is by far the finest specimen of
military architecture in British America. It
was built by Colonel Romer, a famous German engineer, at the country's expense, and
called Castle William. It is a *quarré* sur-
rounded with a covered way and joined with
two lines of communication from the main
gate to a redoubt which is to prevent the
landing. It is well situated near the channel
to hinder ships from coming up to the town,
which must all come within pistol shot of
this battery. It is mounted with one hundred
pieces of cannon, several of which are placed
on a platform near high-water mark so as to
rake a ship fore and aft before she can bring
her broadsides to bear against the Castle, and
some of these cannon carry forty-two pound-
ers. In peace there is an independent com-

pany of fifty or one hundred men, I am not certain which, that constantly are on duty; but in time of war five hundred able men are exempted from all other military duty to attend the service of the Castle at an hour's warning upon any signal given to the Castle of the appearance of any ships and their number. The Castle again warns the town, and, if there be five ships or more in time of war, an alarm is given to all the adjacent counties by firing a beacon. The province has also a galley or frigate well manned in time of war to guard the coast from privateers and to convoy their home trade."

In 1740 the fort was again enlarged and in a manner rebuilt, and the Castle, as it then existed, is the place to which "Sam Adams's regiments" were withdrawn by Colonel Dalrymple after the Boston massacre.

And now all the island is a pretty park, and boys may sail their shingle boats from the shore, or, under certain restrictions, they may go in and swim from the beach; and you can stay here till half an hour before sunset,

14

when you may tell your boatman to bring
you back to South Boston point; or, if you
did not come in the boat, you may take a
trolley car and for five cents each may go
home and tell your mother all that has happened.

IX.

THE STREETS.

It has been intimated, in preceding chapters of this book, that simply by walking in the streets of Boston one gets a sniff of the air of the history of past centuries. Something, not primeval or prehistoric, but old-fashioned or antiquarian, lingers even in the lines of the streets, and it is often recalled in their names. There are antiquaries in Boston who would gladly recall the names of the original days, for whom Boylston Street is still Frog Lane. It is asking too much to expect a return to these names from a Boston like the Boston of to-day, of which a majority of the inhabitants are from emigrants who have come to this country since the year 1840. But the strangers in Boston who will use this book may be glad to have

a key to a few of the names of the streets
through which they will go. It will answer
their convenience best if these names are arranged in alphabetical order.

Adams Street.—There are several Adams
Streets in Boston, and several Adams Places,
Squares, etc. All of them are named from
the first or second President Adams. John
Adams, the first President of that name,
though not born in Boston, lived in Boston
for a considerable part of his early life. His
house was very near the scene of the Boston massacre; the whole neighborhood is
changed so that it is difficult to "dilate with
the right emotion" when one visits the spot,
but it was in Brattle Square, a little below
where the church stood. A house in the possession of the family later occupied the same
site which the Adams House hotel occupies
to-day, and that name may be considered as a
historical name.

Albany Street.—This long thoroughfare
was made at the time when the South Cove,
so called, was reclaimed from the ocean by

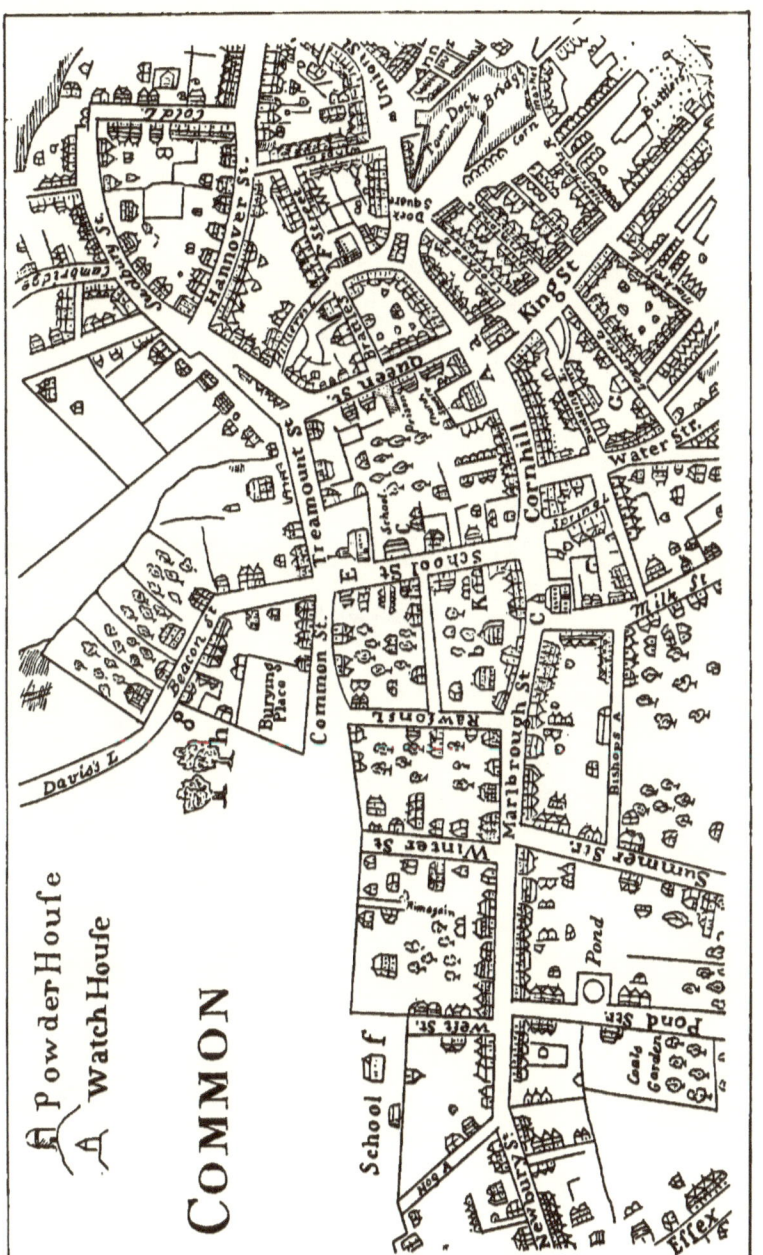

A Section of Bonner's Map of Boston, 1722.

the South Cove Company. It marks, therefore, a period of great enlargement in the
growth of Boston—in particular, the opening
of the Boston and Albany Railway to the
West. The principal streets named at that
time are Albany Street, Hudson Street, Harrison Avenue, and Tyler Street—Harrison
and Tyler being the President and Vice-
President, whose accession to power marked
the first political triumph of the New Eng-
landers in national affairs for many years.

Alger Street, in South Boston, refers back
to Mr. Cyrus Alger, a public-spirited citizen
of the earlier part of this century.

Allston, one of the suburban villages
which is included in the present Boston, is
so named from Washington Allston, the most
distinguished American artist of his time.
Washington Allston lived, however, in Cambridge, not within the present precincts of
Boston proper, and his important historical
pictures were painted there.

Appleton Street is one of the streets upon
what was formerly called the Back Bay. It

is named for the distinguished family of
Appletons, the different members of which
played an important part in the introduction
of manufactures into New England after its
foreign commerce began to decline.

Arlington Street.—The alphabetical names
of the broad streets on the Back Bay were
given by the commission which laid out that
district. For convenience of memory, the
first name is in three syllables, the second in
two, the third in three again, the fourth in
two, and so on till we come to Hereford
Street. The eight names are Arlington,
Berkeley, Clarendon, Dartmouth, Exeter,
Fairfield, Gloucester, and Hereford. The
name Independence Avenue should have
been given to Massachusetts Avenue, for the
purpose of maintaining the alphabet; but
other counsels prevailed. All these names
were taken primarily from towns or places
of an English origin; but, without reference
to this, it may be said that Arlington Street
preserves the memory of the march of Percy
through West Cambridge, then Menotomy.

This place is now called Arlington, a town almost as closely connected as Lexington itself with our early history.

Berkeley retains the memory of Bishop Berkeley, who wrote, " Westward the star of empire takes its way."

Clarendon was named for the Clarendon Press in Oxford.

Dartmouth Street was named in memory of Dartmouth College and of the Earl of Dartmouth, who was the only member of the English Government of Lord North's time who favored the colonists in the least.

Exeter Street was named from Exeter Academy, where so many of the distinguished men of New England have been educated.

Fairfield Street recalls the memory of a distinguished governor of the State of Maine.

Gloucester Street, of the town of Gloucester, which makes Cape Ann and its Revolutionary associations.

Hereford Street preserves the memory of

an English county from which many of the first emigrants to this country came.

In their alphabetical places we will speak of Marlborough Street, Newbury Street, and of the avenues which pass from north to south through the Back Bay. The reader should understand that the whole region thus designated was covered with water in the days of the Revolution, and until the year 1825.

Amory Street preserves the name of the large estate which was divided that this street, with others in the neighborhood, might be laid out.

Anderson Street is a memorial of the Civil War. At the time when Major Anderson was the hero of the moment because he had defended Fort Sumter, the name of this street, in a part of the town especially given up to the colored race, was changed in his honor.

Ashland Street recalls the memory of the days when Henry Clay, who lived at Ash-land, was a candidate for the Presidency.

Atlantic Avenue in its name shows that it is one of the streets reclaimed from the Atlantic Ocean.

Austin Street, in Charlestown, recalls the name of a distinguished citizen of the town in the earlier part of this century.

A Street, B Street, C Street, etc., go back to the time when the region then called Dorchester Neck was annexed to Boston, and first called South Boston. It is on this "neck," so-called, that the fortifications were erected by which Washington and his great subordinate, Ward, drove the English from the town—the last foreign soldiers who ever came to Massachusetts with warlike purpose. This neck was laid out with the natural hope that it might become an important, not to say fashionable, part of the town. It extends into the ocean, and as a summer residence is more agreeable than even the best parts of the old peninsula of Boston. It was laid out somewhat in the fashion of the city of Washington, with cross-streets like those in Washington, named A, B, C, D, etc.,

with a Broadway in the middle, which sought
to recall memories of New York, while the
parallel streets were First, Second, Third,
Fourth, and so on. Historically, the whole
nomenclature of South Boston recalls those
earlier days of the laying out of new cities
and dignifying the streets by systematic
names.

Barton Street recalls the memory of Barton's Point, at the extreme northwest of
Boston, so named probably from some early
shipbuilder.

Battery Street recalls the memory of
fortifications which belonged to colonial
times.

Beach Street, where one may look vainly
for water on either side, was at one time the
beach on the northern part of the South
Cove. This writer has sailed his own hem-
lock-bark boats there.

Beacon Street recalls the name of the
beacon which, from 1636, or perhaps earlier,
stood on Beacon Hill, until, not long after the
erection of the State House, it was taken

away. It has been suggested that this beacon shall be erected again on the new park which the traveler will find between Bowdoin Street, Derne Street, and Mount Vernon Street.

The streets in East Boston were laid out and named between 1830 and 1840. They generally take patriotic names, of which *Bennington* is the first.

The streets at the North End, where they have taken names in more recent times, are generally named from the important towns in Essex and Middlesex Counties, the inhabitants of which come through that part of the town to the city. Such are *Beverly Street* and *Lowell Street*.

In the earlier part of the century the beginning was made of filling up the "Mill pond," by the side of which Benjamin Franklin played; and in 1834 this work was carried on to the north of the causeway which separated that mill pond from the northern shore. *Causeway Street* retains its name, and shows almost exactly the line of the old

causeway which kept the water at the level
of high tide in the mill pond.

Blackstone Street, which is one of the new
streets opening on Haymarket Square, is
named from William Blackstone or Blaxton,
the first inhabitant of Boston of any race
whose history is recorded. *Canal Street* and
Creek Square, in this region, give tokens of
early nomenclature.

After the Revolution, one of the first
tokens of the enlargement of the town was
the laying out of some fine streets which ran
westward down Beacon Hill. These streets
took their names from revolutionary associations, and in some instances they suggest the
names of properties held by those who bore
them. Such are *Hancock Street*, *Bowdoin
Street*, *Temple Street*, named for John Hancock, James Bowdoin, and William Temple.
Belknap Street was named for Jeremy Belknap, the minister of the church in Federal
Street, the founder of the Historical Society,
a person who had always taken great interest
in the history of the colonies. The name of

this street, however, has since been changed to *Joy Street*. *Cambridge Street*, into which all these streets open, took its name as early as 1708.

Boylston Street, as has been said, is the street formerly known as Frog Lane. It was named Boylston in honor of the Boylston family, who won their first distinction from the spirit with which Dr. Zabdiel Boylston insisted on inoculation for the small-pox. This was at the time when the mob of Boston broke his windows, and would gladly have killed him for his enthusiasm in that direction.

Bunker Hill Street, in Charlestown, takes the name of the battle ground.

Canton Street is the first, alphabetically, of a group of streets with geographical names, laid out when the enlargement of the town southward made it desirable that the open lands on or near what was called "the Neck" should be occupied for residences. This neck must not be confounded with Dorchester Neck. It will be convenient to

strangers from other parts of Massachusetts
to recollect that these streets are nearly,
though not quite, in order of the distances
from Boston of the towns whose names they
bear. The streets thus named are Dedham
Street, Canton Street, Brookline Street, Newton Street, Rutland Street, Concord Street,
Worcester Street, Springfield Street, Chester
Square. These names were all suggested by
the fact that Northampton Street next crosses
Washington Street; this had been named
long before. Rutland Street and Brookline
Street break the geographical order, which is
a misfortune. It was once suggested that the
name of Brookline Street should be changed
to Lexington Street, so that it might lead up
properly to Concord Street, but this has never
been done.

Channing Street recalls the memory of
Federal Street Church, in the immediate
neighborhood, where Dr. William Ellery
Channing preached for many years.

The *Common* was so called as early as
1634, when it was bought from William

15

Commonwealth Avenue.

Blackstone, who left Boston at that time. It was bought for a common, from the products of an assessment of two shillings laid on each inhabitant of the town. All those inhabitants had the right to pasture their cows there, a right which they maintained till within the memory of people now living. It is perhaps a question whether the descendants of one of these people might not now successfully claim his right to pasture his beast there. From the Common came the name of Common Street, which was formerly given to all of Tremont Street from Park Street Church. The name still lingers in a short street running from Tremont Street to Washington Street.

Commonwealth Avenue was very properly named when the Commonwealth of Massachusetts reclaimed the deeper waters of the Back Bay, and made land there. It is the central artery of the circulation of the streets then laid out. The names *Newbury Street* and *Marlborough Street* formerly belonged to the great central street of Boston; but as

those names had been given up in order that
the great name of Washington might be
given to the whole of that street, *Newbury
Street*, which is a memorial of old Puritan
enthusiasm, and *Marlborough Street*, which
recalls the times of Queen Anne's victories,
have been transferred to the streets parallel
with Commonwealth Avenue.

Between this region, which marks the
line of daily low-water mark, and the old
upland which belonged to the city, and is
commonly called in local parlance the *South
End*, there was a gore over which the tide
flowed twice a day, and where the titles
were, therefore, different from those of the
city or of the State. This gore was laid
out by a separate company of street makers,
who gave the names of *Columbus Avenue* and
Huntington Avenue to the streets running
north and south, and have taken names comparatively modern for their cross-streets.
Such is the name *Garrison*, a name which
would not have been given to any street in
Boston sixty years ago.

Derne Street commemorates a victory everywhere else forgotten, of which the story is known to the reader. The street is now the western boundary of the magnificent State House, and it makes an interesting memorial of a forgotten victory.

Dudley Street, in Roxbury, preserves the memory of the second governor of Massachusetts.

Edward Everett Square, in Dorchester, preserves the memory of the house, still standing, in which Edward Everett was born.

Faneuil Hall was named from Peter Faneuil, a spirited young merchant who gave the hall to the town of Boston. Faneuil Hall Square takes its name from the hall.

Federal Street was formerly Long Lane. When the convention of the State of Massachusetts met, in the year 1787, to consider the question whether the State would or would not adopt the Federal Constitution, the first meeting was held in the old State House, which is still standing at the head of State Street. The rooms proved not large enough for the purposes of the convention, and they adjourned to meet in what had been "Johnny Muirhead's" meeting - house in Long Lane, not far distant. It is to this incident that the old ballad quoted in Chapter IV refers.

Salem and Essex County were loyal supporters of the Constitution and of the Federal party. They gave the name *Federal Street* to one of the important streets in the city of Salem. In that street also there is a Federal Street Church, and the tune of " Federal Street," now well known, was written by the late General Oliver, who was the chorister of that church, while the minister was preaching one Sunday afternoon.

Fleet Street.—This is one of the streets which take their names from fond recollections of London. The trade with England, for more than a century, was very largely directly with the city of London; and Fleet Street took its name from Fleet Street or Fleet Ditch in London. So close was the relationship between the North End of Bos-

ton and London that, until within the memory of the present generation, its cockney-
isms could be observed in the pronunciation
of the North End. A genuine North Ender
said *weal* and *winegar*, where in another part
of the city people would say *veal* and *vine-
gar*.

The population of the North End has
since twice changed. Once it was over-
whelmed by an Irish emigration; then, about
twenty years ago, this began to give way at
the appearance of a few Italian organ-grind-
ers. The Italians, the Russian Jews, and
the German Jews now occupy nearly every
house in the territory which was formerly
the court end of Boston. An examination of
pupils for the Hancock School in the autumn
of 1896 showed that, of three hundred and
six girls admitted from that neighborhood,
all were from the Continent of Europe with
the exception of a few Arabs. There was
not one girl from England, Scotland, Wales,
or Ireland, or from any part of the American
States. This means that literally the instruc-

tion must begin with teaching these children
the English language. There are a few other
relics of London names. *Cornhill* is one,
which is now given to what was formerly
called New Cornhill, the name of Cornhill
having been originally given to the part of
Washington Street where the newspaper
offices now are, between the old State House
and the Old South Meeting-House. *Long-
acre Street*, which had another London name,
was the part of Tremont Street which passes
in front of the Granary Burial Ground. In
memory again of England, the walks around
the Common are still called Malls by the
old-fashioned people. The first of these
malls was laid out in the last century, and
ran from what is now Park Street Church
southward. It is described in 1790 thus:
"It is on the eastern side of the Common, in
length fourteen hundred and ten feet, divided into walks parallel to each other, separated by a row of trees. On the outside of
each walk is also a row of trees, which agree-
ably shade them." At the present time the

Subway runs under this Mall. Coming into
this century, this Mall was generally called
the Little Mall, while the other malls took
the name Park Street Mall, Beacon Street
Mall, and Charles Street Mall.

Franklin Street commemorates the name
of Benjamin Franklin. But his birthplace
was in the first street north of Franklin
Street, the Milk Street of to-day. It has
been so named certainly as far back as 1808.
This street also probably had its name from
Milk Street in London.

Front Street was so called from its mark-
ing the front of the town, and its eastern
side was washed by the water, or was given
up to wharves for wood and other matters
brought by the coasting vessels. Front Street
took the name of Harrison Avenue in 1840,
when the South Cove streets were named.

The Granary.—Old people still speak
of the burial ground between Park Street
Church and Beacon Street as the Granary
Burial Ground. The town maintained a
granary opposite the Common, where Park

Street Church now is—a common wooden
building, which could contain four thousand
bushels of grain. This property was sold to
the religious society which established Park
Street Church in 1811.

Hamilton Place, nearly opposite, took its
name from Alexander Hamilton, about the
year 1806. In the local history of the eighteenth century and the beginning of the nine-
teenth, a great deal is read of the Manufactory
House. This stood at the head of Hamilton
Place. It was built as a socialistic experiment,
in which philanthropic people united with
the government of the town and sometimes
of the State, in the effort to provide employ-
ment for those not employed in hard times.
It was a handsome brick building, built from
the proceeds of a special excise levied by the
General Court on carriages and other articles
of luxury. It was at first given to the linen
manufacture. The women of the town, rich
and poor, appeared on the Common with
their spinning wheels, and vied with each
other in the dexterity of using them. The

enterprise went forward for three or four
years. The trustees and company annually
attended public worship, a sermon was delivered suited to the occasion, and a contribu-
tion made to aid the business. But the enterprise succeeded no better than similar en-
terprises of 1848 in Paris. Several spinning
schools were established at the same time in
different parts of the town. The best success
of the Manufactory House seems to have been
between 1721 and 1725.

Nassau Street is not the original Nassau
Street, which was a short street, now known
as Common Street. It took this name as
early as 1788, apparently with some reference
to the foreign politics of the time.

Orange Street.—As early as 1708, clearly
from the political conditions of the time, the
old *Middle Street* was changed to *Hanover
Street*, and the highway from the Neck,
leading as far as the late Deacon Eliot's
house, was called Orange Street, in honor of
the Prince of Orange. This became Washington Street when that name gradually

usurped all other names of the main street
of Boston.

The Pound.—In early days the pound
for stray cattle fronted the Common, being
probably, indeed, originally a part of it. It
stood where Houghton & Mifflin's bookstore
now is on Park Street.

Pudding Lane was another London name.
It is the Devonshire Street of to-day.

Queen Street became Court Street in 1784.
King Street became State Street at the same
time, after kings and queens had been abol-
ished.

Rawson's Lane was the Bromfield Street
of to-day. It was named for the provincial
secretary, Edward Rawson.

Salem Street received its name as early as
1708. It is one of those streets which are
named from the region which is approached
by them. Any traveler to Essex County
would have been apt to pass through Salem
Street to take the ferry at the north end
of it.

Salutation Alley happily still retains that

quaint name. It came from the Salutation Tavern, which had a sign of much elegance, representing two gentlemen in the height of fashion, with small clothes and cocked hats, shaking hands. The name is as early as the early part of the eighteenth century. Fortunately, nobody has proposed to change it to any modern name like Fremont or Edison.

The whipping post stood in what is now State Street, near the corner of Devonshire Street. It was removed about 1750. Culprits were whipped near the same spot, on the top of a cage in which they were conveyed from the jail. Public whippings were discontinued about the year 1800.

Sudbury Street, named, as I suppose, from the town of Sudbury, in Middlesex County, was nicknamed Tattle Street a hundred years ago.

Tileston Street, at the North End, recalls the memory of John Tileston, who was a famous schoolmaster at the corner of this street and North Bennet Street. The Eliot School, named for Dr. Andrew Eliot, the minister of this region in the Revolution, stands on the site of Tileston's schoolhouse. Before 1800 the street was known as Love Lane. Young people must not think that this name was purely sentimental; it was derived from the name of Mrs. Susanna Love, who owned the estate on which the Eliot School stands.

The name *Tremont Street* is comparatively new. It is derived from the word Tri-mountain, which was sometimes called Tri-mount and sometimes Tremont in the early history of the town. I say comparatively new, but as early as 1732 it was given to the part of the street which ran from Hanover Street to where Houghton & Dutton's large store is now. The "Orange Tree Inn" was then at the head of Hanover Street.

"*West Hill*," which is spoken of in the earlier books, was at the foot of Beacon Hill, near the water, a little north of Beacon Street. The hill has been so reduced that Charles Street, which runs over the ground, is now nearly level.

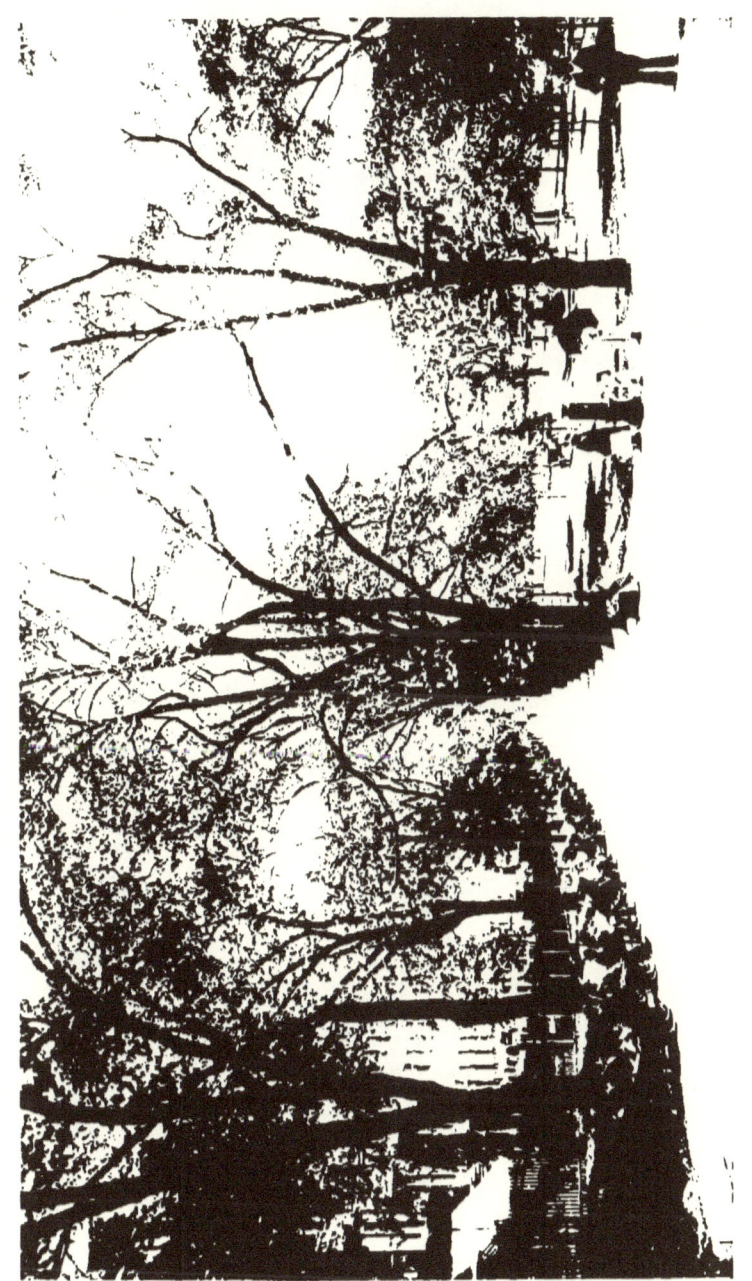

Winnisimet Ferry, which was probably originally *Winnissipit Ferry*, is the ferry to Chelsea, which was then called Winnisimet. Winnissipit would mean " the place of fine streams," and seems a proper name for the junction of the Mystic and the Charles Rivers.

Of the various ante-revolutionary governors there are many memorials in Boston. It would perhaps be dangerous to imply that the popular governors have been remembered and the unpopular ones forgotten. *Winthrop*, the first governor after the great emigration, is commemorated by a statue at the head of Court Street and by the names of several squares, places, and streets. *Dudley*, the second governor, has no statue, but is commemorated by *Dudley Street* in Roxbury, and by an avenue, a place, and a square. *Haynes*, the third governor, has a street and a park named for him. Of *Henry Vane* there is a statue in the public library ; this was studied from a good original portrait of Vane. *Bel*

16

lingham is commemorated by Bellingham Place. *Endicott*, who would seem to deserve a statue, has his name preserved in Endicott Street at the North End. This street was formerly called *The Old Way*.

Leverett's name was early given to Leverett Street. Governor Leverett's house stood where the great Ames Building is now, at the foot of Court Street; and it would be well if a bronze tablet there reminded the passers-by of a loyal man and good magistrate. There is a *Bradstreet Avenue* in Dorchester. *Phipps Place*, at the North End, leading out from Charter Street, preserves the name of the picturesque New England skipper who, while he was governor, knocked down with his own fist the captain of one of the king's vessels. Of *Richard, Earl of Bellomont*, of *Samuel Shute*, and of *Richard Burnet*, all royal governors of the province, there are no such memorials. Bellomont is believed to have lived in the Province House, where he was probably better lodged than ever before in his life. *Belcher*, if there were anything to remember about him, might be meditated on by any one who crosses from Atlantic Avenue to High Street through *Belcher Lane.*

Of all the "royal governors," as we call them, the most distinguished was *William Shirley.* It was under him that Louisburg was taken; it was with him that Washington conferred after Braddock's defeat. He was, indeed, a great war governor. His house, which was an elegant monument of his time, was on Dudley Street in Roxbury; there is scarcely anything left of it now which will interest the antiquarian. Shirley's life has never been properly written, and his papers, if they exist, are hidden somewhere where the historian has no access to them. His name is preserved in a street, not inconsiderable, in the neighborhood of his old house in Roxbury.

Pownall, who was the only royal governor who was really interested in the development of the province, has no memorial which is known to me. *Hutchinson,* who was regarded as a traitor by all the patriots of revolutionary times, deserves rather to be considered as a sort of Hamlet, a man not equal to his position :

> The world is out of joint, O cursèd spite,
> That ever I was born to set it right!

His house was riddled by the mob, but stood until the year 1834. There is a *Hutchinson Street* in Dorchester.

No place has preserved the memory of General Gage or of Sir William Howe, who were the last royal governors of Massachusetts ; and none will.

There is a *Tudor Street* in Dorchester. The determined antiquarian may reflect here that if the Cabots ever saw Boston they saw it when they were floating the flag of a Tudor sovereign. There is no memorial of the house of Stuart in Boston ; there were once portraits of Charles II and James II in the old State House, but General Howe took them to Halifax, and there they appear to have been lost. They are perhaps at this moment moldering in the attic of some Halifax warehouse. The house of Hanover is still remembered in Hanover Street, and the house of Brunswick in the Brunswick Hotel.

INDEX.

THE END.

D. APPLETON AND COMPANY'S PUBLICATIONS.

A PPLETONS' HOME-READING BOOKS.
Edited by W. T. HARRIS, A. M., LL. D., U. S. Commissioner of Education.

This comprehensive series of books will present upon a symmetrical plan the best available literature in the various fields of human learning, selected with a view to the needs of students of all grades in supplementing their school studies and for home reading. **NATURAL HISTORY, including Geography and Travel; PHYSICS and CHEMISTRY; HISTORY, BIOGRAPHY, and ETHNOLOGY, including Ethics and Morals; LITERATURE and ART.**

(*Others in preparation.*)

These books will be found especially desirable for supplementary reading in schools.

D. APPLETON AND COMPANY, NEW YORK.

D. APPLETON AND COMPANY'S PUBLICATIONS.

YOUNG HEROES OF OUR NAVY.

UNIFORM EDITION. EACH, 12MO, CLOTH, $1.00.

THE HERO OF ERIE (*Commodore Perry*). By JAMES BARNES, author of " Midshipman Farragut," " Commodore Bainbridge," etc. With 10 full-page Illustrations.

In this graphic and spirited story Mr. Barnes tells of Perry's adventures as a boy on the frigate General Greene, and conducts his hero through the exciting scenes which attended the battle of Lake Erie. It is a story which illustrates the resourcefulness, energy, and dauntless courage which have characterized our naval heroes from Paul Jones to Dewey and Hobson. The book is an important addition to a series which is indispensable for American youth who wish to know the historic deeds of our navy, and at the present time the Young Heroes of our Navy Series is of peculiar interest to older readers.

COMMODORE BAINBRIDGE. From the Gunroom to the Quarter-deck. By JAMES BARNES, author of " Midshipman Farragut." Illustrated by George Gibbs and Others.

"A well-told story of a gallant captain of the sea. . . . The boys will read it with avidity, and will thank Mr. Barnes for it."—*New York Sun.*

MIDSHIPMAN FARRAGUT. By JAMES BARNES, author of " For King or Country," etc. Illustrated by Carlton T. Chapman.

" We do not know of a more thrilling book for boys, or one more interesting, than ' Midshipman Farragut.' "—*New York Mail and Express.*

DECATUR AND SOMERS. By MOLLY ELLIOT SEAWELL, author of " Paul Jones," " Little Jarvis," etc. With 6 full-page Illustrations by J. O. Davidson and Others.

PAUL JONES. By MOLLY ELLIOT SEAWELL. With 8 full-page Illustrations.

MIDSHIPMAN PAULDING. A True Story of the War of 1812. By MOLLY ELLIOT SEAWELL. With 6 full-page Illustrations.

LITTLE JARVIS. The story of the heroic midshipman of the frigate Constellation. By MOLLY ELLIOT SEAWELL. With 6 full-page Illustrations.

D. APPLETON AND COMPANY, NEW YORK.

D. APPLETON & CO.'S PUBLICATIONS.

*B*OYS IN THE MOUNTAINS AND ON THE
PLAINS; or, The Western Adventures of Tom Smart, Bob Edge, and Peter Small. By W. H. RIDEING, Member of the Geographical Surveys under Lieutenant Wheeler. With 101 Illustrations. Square 8vo. Cloth, gilt side and back, $2.50.

"A handsome gift-book relating to travel, adventure, and field sports in the West." —*New York Times.*

"Mr. Rideing's book is intended for the edification of advanced young readers. It narrates the adventures of Tom Smart, Bob Edge, and Peter Small, in their travels through the mountainous region of the West, principally in Colorado. The author was a member of the Wheeler expedition, engaged in surveying the Territories, and his descriptions of scenery, mining life, the Indians, games, etc., are in a great measure derived from personal observation and experience. The volume is handsomely illustrated, and can not but prove attractive to young readers."—*Chicago Journal.*

*B*OYS COASTWISE; or, All Along the Shore. By
W. H. RIDEING. Uniform with "Boys in the Mountains." With numerous Illustrations. Illuminated boards, $1.75.

"Fully equal to the best of the year's holiday books for boys. . . . In his present trip the author takes them among scenes of the greatest interest to all boys, whether residents on the coast or inland—along the wharves of the metropolis, aboard the pilot-boats for a cruise, with a look at the great ocean steamers, among the life-saving men, coast wreckers and divers, and finally on a tour of inspection of lighthouses and light-ships, and other interesting phases of nautical and coast life."—*Christian Union.*

*T*HE CRYSTAL HUNTERS. A Boy's Advent-
ures in the Higher Alps. By GEORGE MANVILLE FENN, author of "In the King's Name," "Dick o' the Fens," etc. 12mo. Cloth, $1.50.

"This is the boys' favorite author, and of the many books Mr. Fenn has written for them this will please them the best. While it will not come under the head of sensational, it is yet full of life and of those stirring adventures which boys always delight in."—*Christian at Work.*

"English pluck and Swiss coolness are tested to the utmost in these perilous explorations among the higher Alps, and quite as thrilling as any of the narrow escapes is the account of the first breathless ascent of a real mountain-peak. It matters little to the reader whether the search for crystals is rewarded or not, so concerned does he become for the fate of the hunters."—*Literary World.*

*S*YD BELTON: The Boy who would not go to Sea.
By GEORGE MANVILLE FENN. With 6 full-page Illustrations. 12mo. Cloth, $1.50.

"Who among the young story-reading public will not rejoice at the sight of the old combination, so often proved admirable—a story by Manville Fenn, illustrated by Gordon Browne? The story, too, is one of the good old sort, full of life and vigor, breeziness and fun. It begins well and goes on better, and from the time Syd joins his ship, exciting incidents follow each other in such rapid and brilliant succession that nothing short of absolute compulsion would induce the reader to lay it down."—*London Journal of Education.*

New York: D. APPLETON & CO., 72 Fifth Avenue.

D. APPLETON AND COMPANY'S PUBLICATIONS.

www.ingramcontent.com/pod-product-compliance
Lightning Source LLC
Chambersburg PA
CBHW030807020726
47499CB00006B/1808